MADISON'S MESS

SEA SHENANIGANS, BOOK 4

ROBYN PETERMAN

WWW.ROBYNPETERMAN.COM

ACKNOWLEDGMENTS

The Sea Shenanigans characters have been inside my head for a long time and I adore each and every one of them! I can't wait for you guys to read this book. Madison's Mess was a blast to write. Madison and Rick are every kind of nuts and hilarious.

Anyhoo, as always, I write the book, but it takes a whole lot of wonderful people to make the magic happen. I am a lucky girl because I have a whole lot of wonderful people in my life.

Wanda, you rock. Thank you.

Donna McDonald, thank you. You are the most brilliant MYST partner in the world!

My beta readers—Wanda, Susan and Elisa, thank you. I adore you.

And to my readers… thank you. I do this for you.

Steve, Henry and Audrey, thank you. I love you and you make everything worth it.

DEDICATION

For my Mom…
You taught me that the sky is the limit.
I love you.

BOOK DESCRIPTION

What could possibly go wrong when a Mermaid and a Werewolf are sent on a dangerous mission by the drunken, diaper-wearing God of the Sea?

Better question. What could possibly go right?

Madison
Unlike my sisters, I haven't found my HEA. And I'm looking —hard. But finding a man who wants to blowhole dive in Hawaii on the first date is more difficult than you might imagine. I've been forced to settle for a few meaningless orgasms with men who disappear when I suggest fun activities, like scaling twenty stories while blindfolded.

Look, I know meaningless nookie won't help me find my happily ever after, or even a guy who believes tightrope handstands over the Grand Canyon are fun. But there is someone out there for me so next time I do the horizontal mambo, it's for keeps.

May the gods help me. Well, me and whoever I boink next.

Rick
Being a Vegan Werewolf has its drawbacks. I've been exiled from my pack and even the petting zoo of deer, rabbits and raccoons I keep safely tucked away from my fellow Weres isn't enough to banish the loneliness I feel. Talking to myself is becoming dangerous. Just two days ago out of stupefying boredom, I made a wager with myself that I could fly. It didn't end well.

Thankfully Poseidon is sending me on a mission. Unfortunately, it's with a crazy Mermaid who has a worse reputation for death defying recreation than me.

I have no clue what's in store, but may the gods help me. Well, me and this swimming hottie, because I'm totally down.

PROLOGUE

MADISON

"Just another freakin' day in paradise," I muttered to no one as I dipped back down under a crashing wave.

I was playing hooky. I was supposed to be manning the front desk of our tropical island tourist trap, but I decided a forty-two-minute power swim in the ocean would help my frayed nerves. Our tourist business was sucking less than usual. We had a lodge full of both human and immortal guests at the moment. Not real sure who decided picking an island smack in the middle of the Bermuda Triangle was a good plan, but that was exactly what my sisters and I had done a century ago.

And now? Now the Mystical Isle was our home.

"Five more minutes, guys," I told the pod of dolphins that had joined me while I shirked my responsibilities.

The icy cold water on my overheated skin calmed me. Weaving in and out of the waves, I let my tail do most of the work. White foamy caps on the waves burst and slid back into the sea, morphing to a clear teal blue. The feeling of gliding through the salty water was almost indescribable. However, the restlessness I could sense from the sea creatures around me made my swimming almost manic. Moving fast enough was impossible. And I wasn't sure if I was swimming toward the unrest or away. Something strange, or bad, or weird was going to happen... or possibly strange, bad, *and* weird. Kind of like my luck lately.

Was something coming for my island and the people I loved? Or was it coming for me?

I searched the horizon as I floated in my favorite place in the Universe—nothing but clear blue skies and enormous puffy white clouds overhead. My island home was a small dot in the distance. Was there an omen of impending doom in the roar of crashing waves? Was it the agitated behavior of the fish in the sea? Was my imagination working overtime... again?

My shimmering pink tail twitched under the waves as a school of minnows circled me and tickled my scales. Maybe I *was* imagining things. Living forever could do that to a person... or Mermaid, in my case. Remembering to find beauty in the simple things was fast becoming an effort.

Sharing everything with my sisters had made immortality less mundane, but they'd all found luuurve recently—and they were sharing their everlasting lives with their newfound other halves. Tomorrow was my eldest sister's wedding to her idiot Pirate.

Tallulah, Misty and Ariel had all found their HEAs.

Me? I didn't have one of those yet. I wanted one, but finding one was tying my tail in knots. Problem was, I was an adrenaline junkie who wanted adventure, life-threatening danger and to scale twenty story buildings while blindfolded. Finding a man who thought blowhole diving in Hawaii was a good date was seriously difficult.

Whatever. Settling for a few meaningless orgasms here and there with dudes who disappeared when I suggested sky diving without parachutes was going to have to suffice for now.

Wait. No. Maybe I was doing this all wrong... Meaningless orgasms were not going to get me a happily ever after or a guy who thought doing a handstand on a tightrope over the Grand Canyon was no biggie.

Fine. Not a problem. I was no longer going to have sex for fun. Next time I did the horizontal mambo, it was going to be for keeps. Finding a *keeper* might be a challenge, but there had to be someone out there that was as batshit crazy as I was...

May the gods help me, and whoever I boinked next.

1

MADISON

"And so by the power vested in me by the online nuptial course I took last week on me pilfered laptop, I now pronounce ye, Pirate and Purple Swimmin' Hooker," Bonar shouted, raising his fists high in the air and pumping them like the dolt that he was. His puffy shirt had so much material in the sleeves that his face was completely obscured by the billowing yardage as he danced a spastic little jig around the wildly alarmed bride and grinning groom.

The small crowd was silent, surreptitiously glancing around trying to figure out if Bonar was joking or serious. He was serious and seriously looking to get his butt handed to him. Even the glorious surroundings of our lovely little island with the sun setting over the sparkling teal blue sea couldn't negate the truth that the bride had just been called a working girl.

"Holy hell and seashells," I muttered, biting back a grin. We were Mermaids, not humans. A human ceremony was bound to go wrong but I had no clue it would go *this* wrong.

My sister Tallulah had just married Pirate Doug aka *that colossal mess of immortal idiocy* in a human ceremony. The Pirate-Vampire was the very same immortal dimwit who had stolen her heart a century ago. He'd also stolen all of our money because he was a jackass. However, the heart wanted what the heart wanted. Tallulah wanted Pirate Doug and she was getting her wish. Thankfully, he was growing on all of us—mostly like an irritating yet non-fatal rash.

My other two happily mated sisters, Ariel and Misty, glanced over and tried not to laugh. The wedding was turning into a shit show. I had to suck my bottom lip into my mouth to keep from bursting into giggles.

Tallulah most certainly did not need to be called a *purple swimming hooker* on her wedding day. The Pirates had a very bad habit of referring to Mermaids as *hookers*. We were not hookers, occasionally loose in the morals department, but not hookers. The use of the term didn't bode well for the Pirates' lifespans—immortal or not.

It was all I could do not to wiggle my fingers and send a blast of glittering pink magic to set Bonar on fire. The heinous shirt and lacy breeches would go up in flames beautifully. Besides, a little fire might distract from the fact that the questionably qualified *minister* had just called the bride a streetwalker.

Bonar was immortal just like the rest of us. If he lost an arm or leg in the blaze, it would grow back in a few weeks. Granted it would be itchy, but he deserved a little discomfort for the confusing sermon about *eyeliner wearing dingy danglers* and *cod faced tar stains*. The Pirate, who quite accurately referred to himself as an *arse*, was dimmer than a single watt bulb. I was still shocked that Tallulah had agreed to let him officiate her wedding to the brain challenged love of her immortal life, Pirate Doug. But love and great sex did strange things to people.

All three of my Mermaid sisters had fallen head over tail in love in the past several months. It was wonderful even though they'd all three chosen oddballs. Ridiculously, they insisted I was next, but I couldn't for the very long life of me figure out who my happily ever after would include.

"Fabulous ceremony," Pirate Doug bellowed to the crowd. "I shall now bed my hooker."

Tallulah flipped off her groom and decked him. Most of the guests applauded her violent behavior. Immortals tended to enjoy a little brawling at their gatherings.

Ariel giggled and tossed her teal blue locks over her shoulder. "We certainly go for the asshole idiot types."

"Speak for yourself," I chided my youngest sister with an eye roll.

"Umm… I was," Ariel shot back with a laugh as she snapped her fingers and produced two piña coladas with colorful little paper umbrellas perched on the rims of the glasses.

Thankfully, she handed one to me. I downed it in a single gulp. It was difficult for a Mermaid to tie one on, but I was going to try.

Ariel sipped her drink and watched me wince as the brain freeze kicked in. "Want another?" she inquired with a grin.

"Yessssss," I hissed, pressing my fingers to my forehead. "Make it a triple. Watching this wedding end in bloodshed requires alcohol."

"Your turn is next, Madison," Ariel replied, handing me another fruity drink.

I just rolled my eyes and secretly hoped she was right.

Ariel's mate Keith was a Selkie with the maturity level of a fourth-grade boy. However, the big dummy loved my blue-haired sister to distraction and she loved his questionably intelligent ass right back.

Ariel's name wasn't really Ariel—it was Joan. My baby sister had watched *The Little Mermaid* so many times she'd adopted the name. Of course, I had no room to talk. My real name was Cindy. However, Splash was my favorite movie. *Madison* was far superior name to *Cindy*.

"I'm so happy I didn't opt for a wedding," Misty said, joining Ariel and me as we watched our sister Tallulah kick her groom's ass.

Misty's mate was a freakin' demigod—Cupid no less. He wasn't as dimwitted as Keith or Pirate Doug, but he came with his own set of challenges, which included an ego the size of the continental US.

"When you find the man of your dreams, I'd suggest eloping or just living in sin like I do," Misty said, taking the drink out of my hand and swigging it.

"Noted. Anyhoo, I'm not in the market for a keeper. The single life suits me just fine," I lied through my teeth. "I prefer blowing stuff up and bungee jumping."

"Riiight," Misty muttered with a laugh as she quickly made her way toward the smackdown between the bride and groom. Or to be more accurate... the smackdown of the groom by the bride. It wouldn't be a Mermaid-Pirate gathering without a little massacre of sorts.

"Life isn't complete without someone to bungee jump

with," Ariel added with a wink as she too went to separate the bride and groom before we needed a doctor.

"Again. Noted," I said with another eye roll. Having my sisters feel sorry for me made my scales itch. I was perfectly fine being single and lonely. Not.

My sisters meant well. They were all ridiculously happy and wanted the same for me. Pulling on my pink hair, I sighed. Being a Mermaid was all kinds of fantastic and all kinds of sucky at the same time. Living alone for eternity came with its own set of challenges. We were colorful female warriors with healthy sex drives and deadly magical skills.

At least we'd given up the habits of our Siren ancestors. Eating our paramours was *very* old school and seriously gross. Hence the reason being called hookers didn't exactly fly with us.

Our hair and our eyes were set from birth. My color was pink, Ariel's was blue, Misty's was emerald green and Tallulah's was lavender. Each Mermaid's hair and eyes were unique to them and no two were alike. However, the color of our tails changed with our moods and our fashion choices. I always matched my tail—or when in human form, my sarong skirt—to my bikini top.

"Did that arse Bonar make a joke, for the love of everything salty?" Poseidon grunted in confusion. "Not sure if I'm supposed to laugh, clap or twerk. These human rituals are bizarre. And if I'm correct, it looks like my idiot son might not survive his wedding."

"Sadly, Bonar wasn't joking," I told the green-haired, man-diaper wearing God of the Sea with an eye roll. "Bonar's a nard. Pretty sure he has no clue he just insulted the shit out of my sister. As for your son, Pirate Doug is really hard to kill. I've tried thirty-two times so I'm gonna go with serious injury, not death. And if you twerk, I'll zap you bald. You feel me?"

"Is *that* the way you speak to the God of the Sea, Madison?" Poseidon demanded with a raised brow.

"Umm... yep," I replied with a grin. "It's a human rule. All grown men wearing what amounts to an adult diaper with a crown and carrying a scepter are *not* allowed to twerk at nuptial ceremonies. It's punishable by death or baldness."

"My gods, humans are such bloodthirsty bastards," Poseidon hissed, touching the top of his head to reassure himself that his long mossy green—and *way* out of style— hair was still present.

Simply shrugging, I smiled. While the God of the Sea did deserve respect, any full-grown man sporting Pampers and not much else was difficult to take seriously.

"I'm *not* a swimming hooker," Tallulah shouted at the still dancing Bonar as she stepped on Pirate Doug's head. "I'm a Mermaid and I have a name. Do the vows again, Bonar or you'll be dancing the hempen jig."

I didn't even try to suppress my laugh. My sister was the freakin' bomb. All three of my sisters were amazing and I adored them with every scale on my tail. However, even though Tallulah was technically our leader, I was never going to follow her lead if I ever found a keeper and have a wedding. This fiasco was a total shit show.

Bonar, fearing for his life, took another stab at the vows. Pirate Doug seemed thrilled at having had his ass handed to him by my sister. They were a perfectly violent yet loving match. Take two of the wedding began.

I eyed Poseidon who was eyeing me as well. He was my

dysfunctional father figure. When the choices for a dad were slim you went with what was available.

"So when do we dive to the bottom of the sea to repair the tear in the abyss so no more demons slip through?" I quietly asked Poseidon as Bonar tried again.

"We're not," Poseidon whispered in reply as he popped open another bottle of rum while watching Bonar do his best not to refer to Tallulah as a hooker. The God of the Sea was getting progressively drunker. Whatever. He was usually soused. Maybe he was too tipsy to remember we were supposed to dive down and fix the tear… or maybe not.

"Wait. What?" I asked, feeling deflated. Not that I was jonesing to spend time with my de facto father—he was every kind of insane—but I needed an adventure. Being around all the happiness of my sisters was depressing. A little something potentially deadly was necessary.

"It's already done," he informed me, offering me the rum. "Hades owed me for losing the karaoke contest on Mount Olympus last month so I made the evil bastard fix the problem."

"That's not fair," I complained, taking the bottle and downing the rest of the contents. At least it wasn't frozen. No brain freeze this time, just a slight gag. Straight rum wasn't my thing, but this day was not turning out as planned… for anyone.

"Not to worry, my little pink haired Mermaid," Poseidon said, pulling another bottle of rum from his diaper.

I immediately dropped the bottle I was clutching and gagged again. Note to self—wash my hands as soon as possible. How was I to know the God of the Sea carried his alcohol next to his junk? Gross.

"Can you cook?" he asked.

"Yes," I replied, wondering how soused he was.

"What do you think of Gnomes?" he went on.

"They suck."

"Excellent. You're hired," Poseidon told me.

"For what?"

"A shit show of epic proportions."

I stared at the dummy and tried to figure out what plan he had up his sleeve, or in his diaper, since that was all he was wearing. Honestly, I didn't care. If it was dangerous and I could throw daggers at something, I was in.

"I'll take the job."

"Of course you will," the God of the Sea replied with a grin. "What I command is law."

With the smallest eye roll possible, I nodded my head in respect to him. "So what's the mission?"

"The Gnomes are kidnapping lesser gods and torturing them. I need that shit to stop. It's cutting into my golf time," Poseidon explained.

"Mmmkay," I said, glancing over askance at the large freak.

Did he play golf in a diaper? Wait. That wasn't relevant at the moment. It was appalling, but not important. Lesser gods were being tortured by Gnomes. And what the hell did my cooking skills have to do with any of this?

"Not following," I said, still picturing the God of the Sea wearing Pampers at the Mount Olympus Country Club.

Poseidon sighed and let his head fall back on his massive shoulders. "Do I have to explain everything?" he grumbled.

"Umm... yes," I snapped.

"Fine," Poseidon said with a belch and then took another

swig off his bottle. "You will pose as a cooking show star. I've already set that up for you. You're expected on the set of the show shortly. The fucking Gnomes are addicted to cooking shows. You will draw Stew, the Gnome King out of hiding with your beauty and kitchen skills. Once you have him, I'm cool if you'd like to castrate him and skin him alive."

"Ooookay," I said, holding back my bile and wondering if Poseidon had lost his debatably sane mind.

Poseidon went on, oblivious to the fact that I'd paled considerably at the horrifying proposal. "Of course, the de-balling and epidermis peeling is simply an added bonus. What I really want is to get my gods back and to send the Gnomes a very clear message that it's not nice to fool with Poseidon."

"Or Mother Nature," I added.

"What the hell does *she* have to do with this?" he demanded with a shudder. "She's insane."

I really wanted to call *pot, kettle, black,* but decided it wasn't in my best interest. He was correct. Mother Nature made Poseidon look normal.

"It was a joke," I told him as he sagged in relief. "So I'm doing this cooking show alone?"

"Nope," he said as his smile grew wider.

I didn't like that one little bit. Poseidon was always up to no good. "One of my sisters is going with me?" I pressed.

"Nope."

"Care to be less cryptic?" I snapped.

"Do you have a man friend at the moment?" he inquired, not making eye contact.

"What in the Seven Seas does that have to do with

anything?" I demanded as my fingers began to spark with the need to zap the god sky high. It was bad enough that my sisters gave me crap. I didn't need the perennially soused God of the Sea all up in my non-existent love life.

"Nothing," Poseidon replied with a grin. "I'm nosy."

With an eye roll that deserved an Academy Award, I lifted my middle finger to the dolt. His roar of laughter made a few guests glance back at us. Quickly retracting my finger, I narrowed my eyes at Poseidon and waited.

"The mission?" I hissed quietly, getting him back to the matter at hand. I didn't need my sister getting pissed at Poseidon for making me angry. She had her hands full with Pirate Doug and Bonar. Thankfully Bonar had not uttered the word hooker once this time around.

"Fine," Poseidon said, pouting a little. "There's a Werewolf who owes me. At least I think he does." My stomach began to churn. I had a teeny tiny bit of a weakness for hairy howling dudes and Poseidon knew it. "But most importantly, he has a death wish like you do."

My eyes narrowed further and I truly considered zapping Poseidon, but I was smarter than that. "I don't have a death wish."

The huge god tilted his head to the side and stared at me with a raised bushy green brow.

"Fine," I conceded with a drawn out sigh. "I kind of do, but it's the type of death wish where I don't really want to die. You feel me?"

"I do indeed," he replied with a laugh. "This is why I have chosen you. What do you think of Tennessee?"

"Never thought about it," I told him. "Is that where I'm going?"

"Aye. It is."

"It's landlocked," I pointed out. As a Mermaid, I needed water to survive.

"They have tubs," Poseidon countered. "Plus it's where the Gnomes have their main palace."

"They chose Tennessee?" I asked, confused. Of all the places in the world to live, why would Gnomes choose Tennessee? Of course, I was one to talk. My sisters and I had chosen the Mystical Isle—right smack dab in the heart of the Bermuda Triangle.

"Yessssss," Poseidon replied, shaking his head. "Gnomes have no taste. Just get my gods back. You might not know this, but I'm in charge of DIC now. I was voted in—kind of— sort of," he explained with a grimace, downing more of his rum.

I was aghast. It was one thing to carry your booze by your balls. It was entirely another to rule over all the dicks in the Universe. No wonder Poseidon drank so much.

"You're in charge of *all the dicks*?" I choked out. I mean, the visual alone was enough to make me want to grab the bottle of rum and down the entire contents even though it had come out of his diaper. And why did I need to know he was in charge of all the dicks? That was TMI—father figure or not.

"Gods, no," Poseidon said with a bellow of laughter. "*DIC*—Divine Immortal Circuit. All the gods have to take a turn at governing the other idiot gods, demigods and lesser gods. I lost at strip poker a few months back and have to run the damned thing for the next hundred years. It doesn't bode well to have the fucking Gnomes absconding with my gods."

"So that's it?" I asked, aware that it probably was. Poseidon was good at assigning tasks, but not so hot on the details.

"Yep. You leave tomorrow," Poseidon said. "Go hug your sister. I'm going to congratulate my son for making it through his nuptials alive. Oh, and there is no need to let any of the humans you come into contact with know of your species. The Gnomes are fucking idiots. Let them think you're human as well. Do me proud, little Mermaid."

Bowing my head to the God of the Sea, I grinned. We lived openly in the human world—Mermaids, Werewolves, gods, Gnomes and even Vampires. The human realm was very aware that the *Otherworld* existed, but not all were happy about it. "I will. I promise. I'll bring home your gods."

And I would. I never broke my promises. Working with a Werewolf would be a piece of cake as long as he wasn't seriously hot. However, it wouldn't matter how hot he was. I never missed business and pleasure.

Never.

2

RICK

"RICK, MY MAN," POSEIDON BELLOWED AS HE APPEARED IN A blast of salty smelling green smoke.

The son of a bitch startled the hell out of me. This of course, caused my fangs to drop and my claws to burst through my fingertips. I'd almost made the deadly mistake of attacking my uninvited visitor. Instincts were difficult to tame. It would have been one hell of a mistake to assault a god no matter what the circumstances.

Falling off the twenty-foot pyramid of kitchen chairs I was balanced on while trying to shave with a machete, I landed with a thud at Poseidon's feet. Chairs went flying and Poseidon expertly ducked one that came close to knocking his head right off his shoulders. He was lucky he hadn't arrived an hour ago when I was throwing axes blindfolded.

"Holy shit," I shouted as my fangs and claws retracted. Pretty sure I'd wrenched my shoulder out of the socket, I

played it off and glared at my surprise intruder.
Unfortunately, the machete was now embedded in my thigh.
Yanking it out, I tossed it across the room. My leg would
heal in a matter of minutes. I was not a pussy.

"Long time no see," Poseidon went on as if he hadn't just
barely missed being decapitated.

"Can't say that's a bad thing," I muttered, glancing
around to make sure the certifiable God of the Sea was
working solo. The last time he'd paid a visit, he'd brought
his Clam Band—very disturbing. They were basically
human-sized clams with arms and legs—no discernable
faces and they played shitty elevator music.

"Don't be rude, boy," Poseidon chided, making himself
comfortable on the couch in my rustic log cabin loft. "What
exactly are you doing here?"

"Nothing," I replied vaguely. Poseidon didn't make
social calls. My stomach tensed and I crossed my arms over
my chest. It was my intimidating pose.

He wasn't impressed.

"Doesn't look like nothing," the green-haired god
pointed out, nodding at the far wall with ten axes sticking
out of it. "Nice work. All bullseyes."

"Thank you. Did it blindfolded."

"Of course you did," he shot back with a chuckle. "And
why are you living in the middle of nowhere? Shouldn't you
be living at the compound with your pack?"

"I like my solitude," I lied through my teeth.

Basically, I'd been banished. No one thought explosives
in the toilet at the fight-training center was funny. I hadn't
even detonated them. I was hiding them for later to blow up

the three-story dirt hill I'd built. Lupines had no fucking sense of humor. Although, the Alpha's mate flirting with me hadn't exactly helped my case either. And then there was the small issue that I'd wrecked all of the communal vehicles while driving off-road and attempting to jump the canyon in them. However, the topper was when I tried to convince the pack to go Vegan with me. Suffice it to say I was *unpopular* at the moment.

And I was lonely.

Even though I'd amassed quite the petting zoo of deer, rabbits and raccoons to keep them safe from my hungry pack, my pets didn't talk. Chatting with myself was getting old and seriously dangerous. Two days ago, out of stupefying boredom, I'd made a wager with myself that I could fly. That ended badly.

The deer had seemed amused after I'd taken a running leap off the roof of my home and broke most of the bones in my body on the landing. It made me glad I'd saved them. We didn't live in the dark ages anymore. Immortals could shop the organic produce section at the grocery stores just like the humans. We didn't need to ingest Bambi and Thumper.

"I call bullshite on the solitude thing," Poseidon said calmly as he watched my every move.

"You can call whatever kind of *shite* you want, old man," I told him with a shrug of indifference. "I'm quite content being alone."

"Hmm," he replied, glancing around at the disaster that I called home.

It was a fucking mess, but that wasn't unusual for me. I

was an unmated, Vegan, Werewolf adrenaline junky. Plus, I'd given the raccoons free rein. What did he expect?

"Your pack doesn't know how to use your talent," Poseidon said, snapping his fingers and producing a bottle of rum.

That's when I noticed he was only wearing a diaper. Immortals associated with the sea were insanity personified. Well, most of them were. Mermaids were hot. "And you know how to use my skills?" I snapped.

"I believe I do. It's time to pay your debt."

"I already did," I told him with an eye roll.

"Shite," he muttered and slapped himself in the head. "You did?"

"Yep. I took Apollo sky diving and rigged his chute not to open—just like you *insisted*. It was seriously unreal how fast that bastard's limbs regenerated," I remembered aloud and truly still impressed.

Apollo had been furious but quickly realized Poseidon had been behind it. Suffice it to say I now owed Apollo.

Eyeing the drunk old fart, I sighed and ran my hands through my hair. I *had* owed Poseidon, but as I reminded him, I'd already repaid my debt. The green haired bastard had parted the damned sea for my people to escape when we were being chased by our most hideous enemy—the fucking Gnomes.

My pack of Werewolves had been beaten to a bloody pulp by the Gnome bastards and if it hadn't been for the certifiable God of the Sea, I wouldn't even be standing here at the moment. However, I owed him nothing but gratitude now. He would have to live with that.

"Looks like you're growling at the wrong wolf," I said,

straddling a more or less intact kitchen chair and bowing my head. I gave the god the respect he was due even if he was a hot mess in Huggies. The gods were indeed crazy.

"Yes, well, I drink a lot," he replied.

"Understatement," I muttered under my breath.

"My bad," Poseidon said, standing up to leave. "I'll just have to find another insane warrior Werewolf to attack the Gnomes along with the ridiculously gorgeous, unmated, violent Mermaid I've chosen for the job. Enjoy your solitude, Rick."

Solitude sucked. My life sucked. My pets were delightful but kind of boring. Attacking Gnomes sounded like an excellent adventure. I hated those bastards with a passion. And Mermaids? Spending time with a swimming hottie while killing Gnomes was a no-brainer.

Plus, if I did something heroic my pack might let me live within twenty miles of the compound.

"Hang on there, old man," I said quickly before he disappeared.

Poseidon's smug grin grew wide and we both knew he had me.

"Tell me more," I said eyeing him cautiously. The God of the Sea tended to leave important details out.

"Are you mated?" he asked.

"Umm… no. I'm not," I growled. My love life was none of his business. I did just fine in the lady department until they figured out I was into hobbies that occasionally ended in decapitation.

"Can you cook?" Poseidon went on with his bizarre interrogation.

"I can make a sandwich."

The God of the Sea wrinkled his brow in thought. What the fuck was going on here? How was cooking involved with killing Gnomes and potentially shagging a violent Mermaid? Would I lose the gig if I was hopeless in the kitchen?

"I can boil water," I offered. "And I can open bottles with my fangs. I can also use the microwave." I casually moved to block his view of the three charred microwaves I'd blown up. How was I supposed to know you couldn't put metal in the pieces of shit?

"Can you keep your dick in your pants?" Poseidon inquired as he reseated himself on the couch.

"Literally or figuratively?" I questioned, not sure what the right answer was.

"Answer the question."

"Is it a trick question?" I pressed, really wanting to get it correct.

"No, boy," Poseidon bellowed. "Answer it."

Shit. Fine. The truth is supposed to set you free... "I seem to have a difficult time keeping it in my pants," I told him.

"What are your thoughts on Mermaids?"

"Completely carnal." Again, I replied truthfully as my pants got a little tighter.

"And what would you have to say about a pink haired Mermaid, armed to the teeth, and with a death wish stronger than yours?" Poseidon inquired with a grin.

"I'd have to say I'm already in love."

"Excellent," he shouted and tossed me his bottle of rum. "You're hired. Pack a bag. You're going to Tennessee.

"What's in Tennessee?" I asked and then took a healthy swig.

"Your future, Rick. Your future awaits you in Tennessee."

Well, shit. Tennessee wasn't exactly an island paradise, but it sure beat where I was right now. The backwoods of Kentucky were getting depressing.

"I'm in," I said and then froze. "Can you send someone over to take care of my pets?"

Poseidon stared at me as if I'd grown another head. "You're a Werewolf. Werewolves don't have pets. They eat pets."

"I'm Vegan."

The diaper-wearing god scratched his head in confusion for a moment and then shrugged. "I know of a Pirate named Bonar who needs a place to hide out for a bit after performing a human nuptial ceremony where he referred to the Mermaid bride as a hooker. I'm quite sure he'd take a dog sitting job to escape being dismembered."

"Not dogs," I corrected him while trying to follow the bizarre story he'd just shared. I wondered how soused he was at the moment. "Deer, bunnies and raccoons."

Again Poseidon seemed a bit perplexed. I supposed it was a little odd, but my furry zoo had grown on me and I needed them to be protected.

"You have bunnies?" he inquired, trying not to laugh.

I wanted to wipe the smirk off of his face with my fist, but I wanted the mission more. Plus, punching a god in the face wasn't good form. "Yesssss. I have bunnies," I answered through clenched teeth as I willed myself not to smack down on him for enjoying my weakness. "It's a deal breaker if they can't be safeguarded."

With a chuckle and a shake of his head, Poseidon stood

and extended his hand. "Your pets shall be defended until your return. Are you in?"

"Hell to the yes," I replied, taking his outstretched hand in mine.

I had no fucking clue what I was about to do, but I was *totally* in and then some.

3

MADISON

TENNESSEE SUCKED BUTT. THE TUB IN MY HOTEL BATHROOM WAS small. I missed the ocean with a vengeance, but the mission was beginning to reap rewards… kind of. Our show was wildly popular on the local cable access stations in Tennessee and the surrounding states. There were several major networks snooping around and making offers to take the show national. I had no desire to spend my life landlocked as a cooking show star, but I had to admit I was having fun.

We'd done ten episodes and the Gnomes were starting to take interest if their attendance in the studio audience was anything to go by. However, Stew the Gnome King, was a no show so far.

Apparently, my pink hair was all the rage and humans were flocking to the salons to copy my *look*. I was honestly flattered by the fandom. Everything was going well according to the half-assed plan. Well, not everything…

Rick was a serious problem to my sanity and libido. There was no way I was going to boink the Werewolf. I had standards… kind of. I'd promised myself that I was going to keep the next one I poked. I never broke a promise. And I had no intention of *keeping* Rick even though he defined the word insane. He was my co-worker. I *never* peed where I swam.

Shitshitshit.

"Take them off, Mermaid," Rick whispered in my ear, sending sexy chills skittering up my spine.

Ignoring the man I was stuck with for the foreseeable future, I watched the monitor in our dressing room and sized up the audience as I considered the lewd directive. Unfortunately, there was no sign of the Gnome King. And, of course, my wish to be paired with an unattractive Werewolf did not come true… at all.

I eased away from him and sat on the plush leather couch, my eyes still glued to the screen. It was a packed house just as I'd suspected—packed and on the edge of their seats. Which was exactly where we wanted them to be.

"You take yours off," I shot back as I glanced back at him with a raised brow.

If being ungodly beautiful was a sin, he was going straight to Hell when he died—if he ever died, which was nearly impossible. Rick was insane. He'd nearly bit the dust six times in the first week and a half that I'd known him. His future looked bleak for living into tomorrow. Unfortunately, I found that hot.

The idiot made my death wish look like child's play, but I refused to show my admiration. It was all I could do not to jump his hot ass, but Lupines were bad news. *Everyone* knew this. I wasn't stupid enough to let my need for a few massive, wildly satisfying, rock-my-world orgasms outweigh my judgment or self-respect. Werewolves had very long life spans and enormous egos among other large *things*. Plus, we had a mission to complete.

"Would take them off if I could," Rick replied easily with a smug grin that made my damn panties damp. "But I can't. Already going commando. However, if you'd like me to show my goods to the viewing audience, just say the word. Your wish is my command, baby. Always."

"You really are a nard," I replied as I touched up my lipstick knowing he actually had the balls to do it—pun intended. Only ten days with the ass and I wanted to either kill him or ride him until he was blind.

"Thank you," he replied.

"Wasn't a compliment," I shot back.

The werewolf simply chuckled.

"It would make me very *happy* to have your panties in my pocket today."

"How *happy*?" I asked with an eye roll. All he ever did was talk about sex and it was beginning to wear me down. Not that I was about to have sex with the douchebag. He was my partner, not my lover, and I'd promised myself no more meaningless nookie. Mixing business and pleasure got you killed or at the very least made you lose an appendage. Growing back an arm or leg would suck all kinds of butt. We had to take some bad dudes out and return some lesser gods to Poseidon. Regenerating limbs was itchy and could take weeks.

We didn't have weeks. We had days. The Gnomes had now abducted a total of six lesser gods and Poseidon was pissed.

"Having your panties in my pocket is worth an unlimited amount of McDonald's fries happy."

Damn it, I loved McDonald's French fries... Fine. Dumbass wanted to play? I was game. "Works for me. However, it's a thong," I shot back with a naughty grin, hiking up the skin-tight pink skirt I was wearing and stepping out of my lacy wisp of what barely passed for underwear. It was extremely satisfying to hear the cocky jackhole's swift intake of breath. He didn't think I would do it. He was wrong. "*Happy* now?"

"So happy."

I tossed the lace at him and readjusted my skirt. He simply grinned and put them in his pocket. Going commando was nothing compared to what we were about to do on stage. The secret thrill of knowing my panties were in his pocket paled to the stunt I had up my sleeve.

"Finger explosives?" I inquired casually.

"In my pocket. You have the knives ready?" he asked with a wicked gleam of excitement in his eyes.

"I do." I glanced at my reflection in the lit makeup mirror and tried not to laugh.

My expression duplicated his. We were a match made in Hell—a Werewolf and a Mermaid addicted to danger. We'd also been given carte blanche to do whatever was necessary to eliminate our target. Hopefully, the cooking show-loving Gnome King would be in the audience.

"WE GO IN THREE MINUTES AND THIRTY SECONDS," KIM, THE new stage manager, said eyeing us warily. "Are you two... umm... ready?"

"We are," I told her with the megawatt smile that I usually saved for the camera.

Her fear wasn't unwarranted. Kim was the third stage manager in a week. Apparently, Rick and I were too much to handle. It wasn't our attitudes or egos. We kept those firmly in check... or at least I did. We were on time, completely professional and always delivered. Sometimes they just weren't pleased with what we delivered. However, the audience *was* and therein lay the conundrum—for them anyway.

"And you're making apple pies today?" Kim questioned the hushed tone one normally reserved for funerals.

"We are," I repeated.

"Look, Jack and Diane, I'd really like to keep my job. I'm a single mom with bills to pay. Is there anything I should know about the apple pies?" Kim asked, running her hands through her short, spiky red hair.

"She *is* being polite," I told Rick, taking in Kim's slightly terrified expression.

Humans were so edgy. It took a lot for me to remember our fake names, but so far I'd answered every time someone called me Diane.

"She most certainly is being polite," Rick agreed.

I considered how much to share. Keeping it fresh was paramount to our success. Occasionally, I didn't even know what we would do. I just let it happen naturally. Sadly our *naturally* wasn't everyone's cup of tea. However, from what we were hearing, the Gnomes were loving it.

"Fine, Kim. I think I might like you. You're the first stage manager to look us in the eye without stuttering."

"I have a toddler," she told us.

"That explains a lot," Rick said with a nod of approval.

"The apple pies will be flambé," I stated casually.

"Blow torch?" she asked.

"No, but damn it, I wish I'd thought of that," I said, appreciating her more by the moment.

"Fireworks?" Kim tried again.

"Nope."

"Well, I'm pretty sure that you guys are far beyond using a simple lighter… so hit me. How are you going to light the pies on fire?"

Her refusal to back down was refreshing. I could tell *Jack* was impressed as well. The God of the Sea had chosen our aliases—Jack and Diane. Apparently, the soused, green haired, man-diaper wearing god loved John Mellencamp… hence our redonkulous names.

"It would be very helpful to know what you're going to do," Kim said, wringing her hands.

It wasn't an entirely bad idea to tell her. That way she could have the crew ready with fire extinguishers if something went awry. If I used magic to put out a fire, I'd blow my immortal cover.

"Finger explosives," I whispered as her eyes grew wide.

"Seriously?" she asked, popping a few antacids in her mouth.

"As a heart attack," Rick said with a grin that charmed Kim even in her distressed state.

Her blush matched her hair and she self-consciously smoothed out her rumpled and dated business suit.

I was getting used to the effect *Jack* had on women of every age and species. However, it still made my green-eyed inner monster annoyed. He wasn't mine, but he wasn't going to be anyone else's either—at least not when I was watching.

"Thank you for sharing," Kim said, downing a few more chalky tablets. "And that's the extent of it?"

"Of the fire? Yes," I assured her.

"Why do I feel like that's an answer filled with omission?" she choked out, scanning the backstage area for fire extinguishers.

"Because it is," I said with a delighted giggle.

Kim grabbed a boom stand for purchase and tried to find words, but it was too late. The show must go on. "For the love of God, please don't kill yourselves. I'll get fired," she called out as we took our places for our entrance.

"Is she *actually* concerned about us?" Rick asked with a perplexed grin.

"If she is, that's a first," I replied, shrugging as I glanced back at the very nervous Kim. "She's quite unusual. First one in a while who can complete a sentence."

Rick followed my gaze and winked at Kim. "She is odd for a human, my lover. I suppose we'll have to keep an eye on her."

"I'm not your lover," I snapped and tried to keep from laughing. He didn't give up.

"Yet," he replied with a lopsided grin.

Kim rolled her eyes at Jack's statement which gave her ten more points in my book. Any woman who was for the most part unaffected by the over-sexed idiot was a woman I could throw back a piña colada with.

Kim was very interesting... possibly very, *very* interesting. Someone who wasn't cowed by immortals might be useful to us even if she wasn't aware exactly who and what she was dealing with.

"We go in three. Two. One. And... go," the production assistant said, counting us down.

Thoughts about Kim would have to wait. We had a job to do and possibly a studio to incinerate.

Our theme music filled the sound stage and the fabulously terrifying feeling of falling off a cliff without a parachute washed over me. My entire body tingled and I took a deep cleansing breath. Being alive was exhilarating. Being alive while having a penchant for death-defying hobbies was absolutely intoxicating. Getting to go on stage with a hot Werewolf that I wasn't going to bang even though I wanted to made it close to perfect. The idiot had less fear than I did and I thought that was impossible.

"Good evening ladies and gentlemen," the announcer's voice boomed through the studio mic as Rick and I prepared to walk through the curtain and make our entrance. "Welcome to *Bitchin' in the Kitchen'!* Sit back. Relax. And prepare to duck and cover. It's time to say hello to Jack and Diane... two American kids who I'm fairly sure didn't grow up anywhere near the Heartland! They're hip. They're hot and they're in the kitchen with you tonight! Give it up for the cooks who just might fry your brain and possibly burn the studio down!"

"He makes us sound insane," I said to Rick as the production assistants held the curtains back for our entrance.

"If the shoe fits, we wear it, Mermaid," he said as he grabbed my hand and jogged us out to our state of the art

TV kitchen. "Don't decapitate me tonight. I taped *Game of Thrones* and it's a new one."

His grin undid me. Every move he made undid me. He was definitely a problem.

"I'll do my best," I promised as I waved to the ecstatic crowd.

The applause was deafening and it fed my need for excitement. But sadly applause wasn't enough. I briefly wondered if anything would ever be enough. We needed far more than applause and hopefully we were about to get it.

4

RICK

"YOU WANNA EXPLAIN WHAT THE FUCK THAT JUST WAS?" DAVE, the line producer, demanded, sweating profusely and pulling on his sparse hair. "While these stunts are great for the ratings, the insurance company pulled out."

Unfortunately, Dave reminded me of the Alpha of my pack. Dave was human and weighed in at about three hundred and ninety pounds of mostly fat and he liked to yell. My Alpha spent an inordinate amount of time shouting at me. Dave made me feel right at home. However, I wasn't pleased that he yelled at the Mermaid who refused to admit she was mine.

Kim nervously stood next to our irate bulbous producer and rocked back and forth on her feet. The human woman wore a cross between a pained smile and a rather unattractive wince on her face. To be fair, I didn't blame her. Madison *aka Diane* had almost impaled me with a ten-inch dagger. It was fantastic.

"The insurance company pulled out again?" Madison asked, feigning shocked surprise.

She continued removing her eyeliner. Clearly, it made her concentrate. Concentration would help her not to laugh. Her laugh undid me. Hearing Madison giggle was almost as good as blowhole diving in Oahu, Hawaii.

I was having a *hard* time concentrating—pun intended.

Of course, it didn't exactly help my sanity that every move the Mermaid made ensured that I had a permanent boner. I had a feeling Poseidon had set me up to fail. Keeping it in my pants was almost impossible—not that I'd told him I could. If I remembered correctly, I told him keeping it in my pants wasn't one of my stronger suits. Madison was as violent and as insane as promised. I'd never come across a more perfect female specimen in my three hundred years.

And although I used all my charms on the gorgeous Mermaid, I'd been sleeping solo since I'd met her. Actually, I hadn't slept much. The sheer number of cold showers I'd taken precluded getting any sleep. Trying to keep some blood in my brain instead of my dick was fast becoming a full-time job. Not that I minded going after Gnomes and blowing up things for a TV show, but lack of sleep would make me sloppy at some point. Destroying the Gnomes was a necessity. They were lowlife bastards and ending Stew would ensure my place back in my pack.

However, the more time I spent with Madison, my pack didn't appeal as much as it used to.

I wondered if she liked bunnies.

"Hell, yes the insurance company pulled out. Knife throwing on live TV is considered uninsurable—not to mention the fucking finger explosives," Dave shouted, turning as purple as I'd ever seen him in the short time I'd known him. "So, if you'd lay off on the near decapitations, we could possibly work a deal for a bond."

"No can do," I said as the hair and makeup gal wiped my face clean of the makeup I'd worn for the camera.

Not that I needed any. I was gorgeous as most Werewolves were—blue-eyed, blond-haired, ripped and batshit crazy. Madison simply needed to realize we were a match made in Heaven.

Or Hell if you asked Dave.

"Dave," I said gamely as I nodded politely to the nice human woman who groomed me daily. If I wasn't mistaken —*and I wasn't*—Madison didn't it like when I charmed the ladies. She liked me more than she let on which was excellent. "The audience expects the unexpected from us. If we can't throw knives, start fires and basically try to kill each other we'll disappoint our fans. We'd really hate to disappoint our fans. However, I do have an idea."

"Is it legal?" he asked, grabbing Kim's bottle of antacids and swallowing a few.

"Define legal," I shot back with a grin.

"Fuck me," Dave muttered as he sat on the couch in defeat. "What do we need?"

"An airplane, one hand held camera, two go-pros, two parachutes, two cups with lids and the fixings for a smoothie," I replied evenly.

"Yesssss! I'm in," Madison said with a wide grin pulling at her sexy mouth.

"Shit," Dave muttered. "I'll see what I can do. Kim," he

snapped at the poor harried woman. "Go see what you can do."

"Yes, sir," she whispered, paling considerably. "Is this safe?"

"Of course it's not fucking safe," Dave bellowed. "Just go see if we can make this death wish happen."

"Will do," Kim stuttered as she sprinted from the room.

"You're gonna give me a heart attack," Dave groused, mopping the sweat from his brow and lighting up a cigarette.

"Nope, Dave," I shot back. "You're doing just fine without our help."

"WERE YOU SERIOUS?" MADISON ASKED AS SHE STARED OUT OF the window in the swanky hotel suite the studio had provided for us during the shoot.

Sadly the suite had two bedrooms—mine and hers.

"About what?" I asked, scanning the maps and checkpoints on my laptop. Poseidon had supplied some intel about a certain bar the Gnomes liked.

"Being human blenders."

"Come again?" I said, trying to pinpoint the target. The bastards seemed to frequent human bars in town—not in their Gnome form but in their human form, which was just as disgustingly unattractive. Apparently, the Gnome Palace was somewhere in the area too.

"Would if I could," she muttered under her breath thinking I wouldn't hear her.

But I did hear her and it made my pants tighten to the point I was sure my dick was choking to death.

"Sorry. I missed that," I said with a wide grin, pinning the hotter than Hades Mermaid with a loaded stare.

Madison glanced over in surprise. The Mermaid was wearing something she called a *sarong* and a bikini top. When we were away from the human population she wore what she liked to call her comfy clothes. I called them *boner* clothes. Clearly, she was unaware of Werewolf hearing abilities. I could hear a pin drop a mile away.

"Umm... nothing, dorko," she said with a blush that matched her gorgeous pink locks. "I was referring to the sky diving catastrophe you pulled out of your ass after the show this evening."

"You think it's a bad idea?" I asked, perplexed. Earlier in the afternoon, she'd split apples balanced on my head with daggers and we'd set fire to the pies with explosives. How could she think sky diving was bad?

"Nope," she said with a giggle. "It's horrifyingly fantastic, but there won't be a live audience. Hence no chance to nab the Gnome King."

"This is true," I replied, sitting on my hands so I didn't grab her and sprint off to my bedroom in the suite. It was all I could do to keep my eyes on her face instead of her fabulous knockers. "However, since Stew hasn't bothered to show his ugly mug, we can case the area from the plane and suss out the location of the Palace. If the fucker doesn't come to us, we shall pay a visit to him."

"Dude, my face is up here," she informed me with an eye roll.

Shit, I'd failed. She was correct. My eyes were glued to

her outstanding knockers. "My bad. It's just that your, umm… chest is a work of art."

She bit down on her full kissable lips to hide her smile. Yesssss. Point for me. I was proud that I'd said chest instead of hooters or gazoongas.

"Rick, Rick, Rick," Madison said in a serious voice that I hadn't heard yet.

Her tone didn't bode well for me getting to see her boobies. Damn it, maybe my complimenting her girls wasn't my smoothest move. Normally, I didn't have to think twice, the ladies threw themselves at me. However, the Mermaid knocked me off my game.

"Yes?" I asked, wondering if she still had a few knives on her. I never knew where I stood with the Mermaid which was sexier than her knockers.

Madison sighed and sat down on the edge of the desk where I was working. Her delectable scent made me a little dizzy.

"Here's the deal. If I bang you, I have to keep you. I made a promise to myself to stop having meaningless sex with losers. You're not a keeper, dude," she said with a sad smile.

"Why is that?"

"Well, for one thing, you've come close to death a half dozen times this week," she said.

"While this is true, I'd like to point out that you were the cause of nearly all my near-death experiences," I said carefully, watching her hands to make sure she didn't go for a weapon. Her knife skills were a huge turn on for me.

Madison scrunched her nose and considered my

statement. "Excellent point. And you almost beheaded me three times."

"Does that upset you?" I asked.

She grinned and shrugged. "Not really. Does it upset you that I almost took your eye out with a throwing star?"

"Not at all. The only time I was a little iffy was when your dagger grazed my Johnson."

"That was a total accident. I got distracted by the excitement in your..." she faded off, smacked herself in the head and blushed again.

"In my pants?" I offered with a laugh.

"Yesssss," she said with a giggle and an eye roll. "The excitement in your pants. It was... impressive."

Closing the laptop, I grabbed her hand and led her to the couch. Keeping a safe distance between us so I didn't accidentally put my hands on her girls and end up getting stabbed, I settled myself on the far end of the sofa. I wanted the Mermaid more than I wanted to go wingsuit flying, but I needed her to be onboard.

"Here's how I see it. You're completely fucking certifiable and I'm one hundred percent insane," I began.

"Umm... is that how you get the girls? It's kind of a jackhole way to start," she said, squinting her sparkling rose-colored eyes at me.

"It is?" I asked, confused. I thought the truth was supposed to fucking set you free...

"Yep, but keep going. I'm curious how far you can shove your foot up your ass before it comes out of your mouth."

"Not a problem," I said with confidence. "I don't really date... or I do, but it's always over before it begins," I admitted, realizing my statement sounded as pathetic as my life had become living with bunnies, deer and raccoons.

Shit.

"Mmmkay," Madison said tilting her head to the side and pursing her lips. "You're hot. Your ass is to die for. You are kind of a nard, but you seem to have a party going on in your pants. What's wrong with you?"

"Are you serious?" I asked, grinning from ear to ear.

"You're happy I called you a nard?"

"Absolutely. It doesn't bug you that I like zorbing?"

"What in the gods' name is zorbing? Is it dangerous?" she asked as her eyes lit up and my Johnson almost burst out of my jeans.

"Imagine climbing inside a fucking enormous plastic ball —hamster style, except human-sized," I explained, beginning to bounce on the couch a little. "You go to the highest dang hill you can find and let that sucker roll."

"Holy hell and seashells," Madison said as she too began to bounce.

It was time to really impress her.

"Some losers like to be strapped in, but not me," I bragged. "I free willy that ball."

"That is so freakin' hot," Madison said, scooting closer.

"That's nothing," I replied, inching my way toward the goddess of my dreams. "I could take you to the hike of death in Huayna Picchu, Peru."

"Duuuuude, have you ever been blowhole diving in Oahu, Hawaii?" Madison shouted with glee.

All the blood in my brain was now in my pecker. She was perfect. Why wasn't I a keeper? I sure as hell wanted to keep her. I didn't know if the two of us together would live to see tomorrow, but it would be a hell of a great death.

Not sure I could make a coherent sentence, I gripped the edge of the couch like my life depended on it and thought about the horrific time I saw my grandmother naked when I was twelve. My Willy deflated and I was back in control. As long as the Mermaid didn't touch me, I was pretty sure I could speak.

"Blowhole diving in Hawaii is one of my favorite things to do," I said, wincing as the image of my granny's hooters was still stuck in my frontal lobe.

"Shit," Madison said with a long sigh.

"What?" I asked, mentally damning my granny's still present tits to hell.

"Okay," Madison said, jumping up off the couch and pacing the suite. "I really want to boink you, but if I do, I have to keep you." She pulled on her wild pink locks and continued to pace. "Your lack of a fear gene is appealing—almost as appealing as your ass."

My desire to throw Madison over my shoulder and boink her blind was making me sweat.

"However, I've never been in a relationship that worked."

"Neither have I," I volunteered in my outdoor voice. "I suck at relationships. SHIT," I bellowed. That probably was *not* the right thing to say when I wanted her to keep me. "I meant I've very good at sucking... umm... stuff."

Letting my head fall to my chest, I again pictured my granny's sagging bosom to punish myself. Clearly, I'd been living with bunnies for too long. My verbal skills were appalling in her presence.

Madison laughed and paused her pacing. "It's cool. I suck at relationships too… and I'm also *very good* at sucking things."

I was pretty sure my eyeballs rolled into the back of my head and I forgot how to breathe.

"Soooo, this entire conversation might be moot because there's a fine chance that we'll either kill each other in the next few days or the Gnomes will do it for us, *but…*," she said, looking wildly unsure.

"But?" I choked out, still trying to make my lungs work after her admission of her excellent sucking skills.

"*But* the one thing I think I've neglected in the past was getting to really know someone before I banged them blind. I think the logical thing to do before I boink you sightless—if it comes to that… no pun intended—is to date."

"You mean like throwing shit at cars, TP-ing my Alpha's house and making out in the back of my SUV?" I inquired. I had very little experience of actually dating as my reputation for being a daredevil with a death wish preceded me.

"Umm… no," Madison said with an impressive eye roll. "I mean date as in taking me to dinner first before we do that other shit."

"I'm down with that," I shouted, pumping my fist in the air. "You wanna go get a salad?"

"Are you implying I'm fat?" my Mermaid hissed and produced a wicked looking dagger out of thin air.

"Holy shit, that's hot."

"It won't be as hot when it's embedded in your forehead," she pointed out correctly with her eyes narrowed to slits.

"True," I agreed readily and then wondered for the

umpteenth time of the truth would set me free or result in a bloodbath. "I... umm... I'm a Vegan," I whispered so softly that I almost couldn't hear myself.

"Didn't catch that, butthole," Madison said, still aiming the knife at my head.

"Fine," I grumbled. "I'm a Vegan. I don't eat meat or any animal products."

Her jaw went slack. "But you're a Werewolf."

"It's a life choice," I explained, ready to dive behind the couch if she felt the need to stab me for being a freak of nature.

Madison paused and thought it over. "*Your* life choice?"

"Not exactly," I admitted. "I choose to save the lives of all the living and breathing furry creatures that don't deserve to be eaten. Plus a plant-based diet will help you live longer."

"Umm... you're immortal," she reminded me.

Shit. She had me there. I mean, we could die, but not by any kind of human standards.

"Right," I said with a lopsided grin. "I guess it is my life choice."

Madison's smile grew wide. Her pink eyes sparkled and I was pretty dang sure I was staring at an angel.

"I can live with that as long as I can have some French fries with my salad."

"Deal," I shouted.

Life was very good right now.

I just hoped we would make it to tomorrow.

5

MADISON

DAMN IT IF THE NARD WASN'T GROWING ON ME IN A BIG BAD way. He was funny and kind of sweet in an idiotic manner. Not to mention, he was hotter than Hades in July. *And* he wanted to take me zorbing. Maybe boinking my co-worker would be okay... once or twice or eleven times. I did enjoy breaking rules.

"So tell me this," I said, stuffing French fries into my mouth as we sat in his parked truck casing a bar that Gnomes were known to frequent. "You got kicked out of your pack?"

"Kind of," Rick replied, sheepishly grinning at me while he ingested his fourth salad in as many minutes. "I'm a liability."

"That's bullshit," I snapped, dipping my fry into the ranch dressing he refused to eat since there was buttermilk in it. "You're just adventurous—like me. My sisters would never banish me for blowing up stuff. Actually, all four of us like to blow up stuff."

"You're really lucky, Madison," Rick said with a sad smile. "I would be so fucking happy if my pack liked to bungee jump and ride motorcycles blindfolded. Mostly they play cards and eat."

I was silent and willed myself not to blurt out an invite to the Mystical Isle. Rick would fit right in with the rest of my insane crew. However, I didn't know him well enough to boink him yet. I certainly wasn't going to invite him home to be terrorized by my family until I'd banged him. I wasn't an idiot. I had to fall in love with him first and I had no clue what that felt like.

"So you think Stew will be at the bar?" I asked, getting back to business.

Rick shook his head. "Nope, the King rarely mixes with humans. But if we trail the jackasses that are there, we can possibly learn the location of the Gnome Palace."

Sweet Poseidon on a bender—the Werewolf was smart too. Crap.

Humans milled in and out of the bar. It was only ten in the evening. The bar was open until midnight. Normally I would have been bored to tears but sitting in tight quarters with Rick was anything but dull.

"You know, this kind of fun," I said as I hunkered down his truck and waited impatiently for our mark to come out of the seedy bar in the scummiest part of town.

Checking for the knives and explosives in my pockets, I finished off the rest of my fries. I was kind of sad that we weren't going to TP his Alpha's house, but the night was young. Rick's pack was only an hour and a half away from where we were in the armpit of Tennessee.

"Ridding the world of trash for a soused god who wears

a diaper is definitely high on my list of a good date at the moment," Rick said with a panty-melting grin that made me giggle.

I didn't have the heart to tell him that as far as dates went it was kind of weird, but he was kind of weird. And if I was being honest with myself, I was weird too. I'd racked up plenty of bland dates in my centuries on earth. The kind of girl who liked fancy restaurants and then an hour at a jazz bar drinking expensive wine wasn't me. I'd rather walk on the ledge of a twenty- story building and then throw back a few piña coladas followed by a swim in the ocean with some sharks.

Rick began to squirm in his seat. I was already aware that his movement meant he was about to say something— usually something wildly and fabulously inappropriate.

"So, should we suck face or something to kill time?" he asked, plastering himself to the driver's side door in case I decided to stab him.

It was incredibly cute and hot… and cute.

"You're delivery leaves a lot to be desired," I said, moving closer.

"For real?" he asked, his eyes going wide with desire as I inched closer.

"Yep," I said as I got near enough to feel the heat coming off his sexy body. His scent was positively erotic. "Terrible choice of words, but really good idea."

"Yesssssss," Rick hissed as he grabbed me and yanked me against him.

Thank the gods his truck was huge. Never in my life had anything felt so good as his hard pressed against my soft.

"Umm… do fangs freak you out?" he asked, slapping his

hand over his mouth. "They like to pop out when I'm horny."

"Are you horny?"

"Very," he said with a chuckle from behind his hand. "I've had a boner since the moment I laid eyes on you."

He was every kind of uncouth and I loved it. "Lemme see," I said as I gently removed his hand. His fangs were sexy and then some. "Me likey. Just don't bite me. Cool?"

"Right. No bite," he stammered, so excited I almost laughed.

He was like a high school boy—all nervous and adorable.

And then suddenly he wasn't. Oh my gods. He wasn't a high school boy by a long shot. The Werewolf had *moves*.

"Gorgeous," he muttered against my lips as my girlie parts revved up with a vengeance.

I'd expected to be devoured. I was so very wrong. His lips were full and firm. His tongue darted out and traced my bottom lip with reverence.

"Holy seashells," I whispered as I wrapped my arms around his neck and nipped at his lips. "You taste so good."

"Better than French fries?" he inquired with a chuckle as his mouth began to explore my neck and collarbone.

"Much better," I gasped out as his razor-sharp fangs grazed my shoulder sending happy chills all through my body. "What happens if you bite me?"

Rick pulled back and grinned. "You're mine then. You'd have to keep me. Forever."

"Okaaay," I said, warming to the crazy idea. "While I find it intriguing, I'm not ready for that. You feel me?"

"I feel you and you feel good," he said as his bright blue

eyes hooded with undisguised lust and his hands found my perky girls.

Gods, I was tempted to yank my shirt over my head, pull my pants off and straddle the Werewolf. My skin was on fire and the thought of seeing him naked was intoxicating. I would have stripped in a hot second if we weren't parked in a public area. I was clearly not to be trusted with my own judgment—at all. A hot Werewolf and a horny Mermaid who liked blowhole diving were a combustible combination.

"Gods, I want you so bad," he said against my neck. "But I'll wait until you decide if I'm a keeper."

"Dude," I choked out, trying to hold my shit together as I arched into his expert hands. "You have to decide if I'm a keeper too. This is for both of us."

"Already decided," he said as his mouth found my nipple. "I'm gonna do the sucky thing. Cool?"

"Yesssss," I said, wriggling my body in delight. "I'd be very cool with that."

"Okey dokey," he said with a sexy smirk and took a quick look back at the bar. "What the *fuck*?" Rick snarled, glaring out the front windshield.

"What is it?" I asked as I straightened my clothes and moved back to my side of the car. What the fuck was right. This couldn't be right. "Is that who I think it is?" I asked, leaning forward to make sure.

"Yep," Rick growled as his claws popped out from his fingertips.

I knew shit was about to go down, but the claw thing was seriously hot.

"Can you control that?" I asked, pointing at his hands.

He nodded and kept his eyes on the developing issue. "Yep. Just getting my weapons ready."

Again. Hot.

"Who are the three men?" I asked, sizing up the enemy. They were enormous and ugly.

"Gnomes in human form," he said quietly. "You think she's with them willingly?"

"I have no idea. You think she has her antacids with her? Ol' Kim the stage manager is gonna need them if she deals with Gnomes."

"Gnomes have nothing on Werewolves and Mermaids," Rick said with a wide grin. "You ready to rumble?"

"We're gonna take them out here?" I asked, as my excitement ramped up.

"Nope. Too public. We're gonna play idiot human cooking show stars who spotted their buddy the *stage manager*."

"It's a dang good thing we have to work right now," I said, admiring the crazy man sitting next to me.

"Why's that, beautiful?"

"'Cause I'm about ready to do you," I admitted with a giggle.

Rick's moan of desire was music to my ears. "That was not very nice of you, Madison. I think my balls are about to explode."

"Shit. Seriously?" I asked, feeling really bad.

"No worries," he said with a pained chuckle. "If they do I can grow new ones."

"Being immortal is really awesome," I said, planting a quick kiss to his lips.

"You bet your sweet ass it is," he replied, adjusting his junk in his jeans.

"Your balls okay?" I asked with a wince.

"Balls are iffy," he said with shrug. "But if I can be with you, my balls can go to hell for all I care."

"That was hot," I told him.

"It was?" he said with a grin. "I wasn't sure, but it's the damned truth."

"The truth will set you free," I promised. "Let's go see if Kim wants to be free."

6

RICK

"Wait," I whispered, grabbing Madison's hand as she started to cross the pitted gravel parking lot. "Stay here for a minute. Can you hear them?"

We weren't all that far from the foursome, but there were about ten cars parked randomly between them and us in the lot. From where we stood, we wouldn't be noticed. They were busy... and loud.

She nodded. "I can. My hearing isn't as good as yours, but they're yelling."

"Face me and pretend we're making out," I instructed as I pulled a ball cap from my back pocket, twisted her hair up into it and secured it on her head. She was too recognizable with her sexy pink locks. I was very aware she could kill the shit out of practically anything, but I couldn't help my need to keep her safe.

Madison made a face and I grinned. "Do we have to *pretend* to make out?" she asked quietly.

"We do," I told her with a slight wince. "If we want my

nuts to come through the evening unscathed, then we need to pretend."

Madison wrapped her arms around my neck and put her face close to mine. For a brief moment, I forgot my own name. The Mermaid had cast some kind of kick-ass spell on me or maybe I was falling...

No. Wait. Didn't have time to go there right now. I needed to concentrate on the business at hand. Figuring out if I was in love was going to be difficult. I'd never been in love.

Lust? Yes. Love? Nope.

"She's giving them an envelope," Madison whispered as she turned her head to watch the unfolding action. "Is she paying them?"

"Looks like it," I said flatly. "How in the hell is stage manager Kim messed up with the Gnomes? She seems so... *human.*"

Madison and I watched as the largest Gnome counted the money and then shoved Kim violently into the crumbling brick wall of the building. Kim put her hands up as if she was used to being struck by the abomination.

"I can't pay any more than I've given you," Kim said in a choked voice as she continued to cower.

"Tough shit," the Gnome growled as he pocketed the envelope. "You pay or *it* dies."

Kim stood taller and got up in the asshole's face. She was either brave or had a larger death wish than Madison and I put together. The Gnome could snap her neck without breaking a sweat.

"*It* has a name," she hissed. "*You* will use it."

"No can do, *whore,*" the Gnome grunted as he again

shoved the breakable human woman against the wall. "You pay or we slay."

"Something is way wrong over there," Madison said softly as her fingers began to spark and singed a hole right through my t-shirt. "Shit. Sorry. If you want to, you can scratch me with your claws. We'll be even then," she said with a small smile.

She quickly patted out the fire and I grinned. My violent little gal was a wonder that never ceased. Gods, I *really* hoped she liked bunnies.

"No worries, baby," I said. "The burn was good. Took my mind off my pecker."

"I won't have any more money until next week," Kim told the irate Gnome in a shaking voice. "This was the deal we made."

"Deals change," the bastard growled and lifted his hand to strike her.

Madison hissed and yanked me behind the truck as she waved her hand and caused the gutters to fall off the building and knock the fucker out cold. Kim screamed and took off running as the other two Gnomes went to aid their unconscious asswipe of a friend.

"There was no fucking way I was going to stand by and watch him hit her," Madison ground out through clenched teeth. "That is total bullshit."

Her fury was so sexy, I almost jumped her in the parking lot. Instead, I conjured up the image of my granny's hooters again. I couldn't allow myself to be controlled by my Johnson. Shit was going down and I needed to be completely present in the moment.

"That was perfect," I said, peeking around the truck to

see if the gutter had decapitated the bastard. It was the only way to kill a Gnome. Well, it was the only way to kill most immortals. No one I was aware of could regrow a head.

"I have no clue if Kim is a bad guy or a good guy at this point, but that son of a bitch wasn't going to backhand her on my watch," Madison grumbled.

"They're gone," I said, pulling her to her feet and opening the passenger door. "Get in. We need to pay Kim a little visit."

"Do you know where she lives?" Madison asked.

"Shit. No," I said with a shake of my head. "Do you?"

"Nope, but Dave will. I'll just tell him we're sending her flowers to make up for the finger explosives we used today and need her address."

"You're sexy *and* smart," I said with a grin.

"I was just thinking the same thing about you," she shot back.

She was definitely a keeper. I just hoped my Mermaid was beginning to feel the same way.

"DAVE WAS KIND OF PUT OUT THAT KIM IS GETTING FLOWERS and not him," Madison said with a laugh as she ended her call.

"Seriously?" I asked with a grin as I put the address into the GPS.

"Yep. So I guess we should send him something too," she said with a wicked little grin. "Thoughts?"

"Umm… silk boxers with our faces on them?" I suggested and then gagged. Now I had Dave's balls in my head along with my granny's hooters. "Strike that. I want my face nowhere near his junk."

"Ditto," Madison said with a shudder. "How about a case of Tums? Or maybe a case of whoopee cushions or chocolate buttholes."

"Shut the front door," I shouted and laughed. "Chocolate buttholes are a real thing?"

Madison nodded and bounced in her seat. "My sisters, Misty, Ariel and I gave a case of them to our new brother-in-law, Pirate Doug, as a wedding gift. They're not real buttholes," she clarified quickly as she shook with laughter. "Just shaped like a butthole."

"You did not." I couldn't get over how perfect she was. How many girls would send chocolate assholes to someone? Most women I knew wouldn't even utter the words chocolate and butthole in the same sentence. An unfamiliar and bizarre tingle washed over me. I was having a lot of strange feelings around my Mermaid. Was this what love felt like? If it was, it was freakin' awesome... and tingly.

"Trust me," Madison said with a wink. "The gift fit the recipient. I think Dave has earned some edible buttholes. Agree?"

"Absolutely."

"Done," she said as she punched the order into her phone and then turned serious. "Do you think Kim is a key player in this shit show?"

I shrugged and watched the road. It was dark and I was carrying very precious cargo—not that an accident would kill us, but I didn't want a scratch on her perfect body. "It's far-fetched to think Kim's involved with the abductions and torture of the lesser gods, but honestly at this point I have no clue."

Madison sat quietly for a moment, I could tell she was thinking as her knees bounced a mile a minute. I was starting to notice all sorts of her sexy little quirks and I liked them.

"Maybe she borrowed money from the Gnomes," Madison said, trying to piece together a motive for what we'd just witnessed. "She told us she was a single mother. Maybe there's something wrong with her child and she needs money."

"If she borrowed money from those fuckers it was a really stupid move on her part," I said, wondering if the human was indeed that stupid or if her situation was that hopeless.

Madison shrugged. "Desperate times can call for really farked-up measures. But if she can get up in a Gnome's face, it makes sense why she could look us in the eye and not be intimidated."

It was curious how much Kim might know of the *Otherworld*. We didn't live in secret, but we kept many secrets from the humans. "I don't think it's a loan she's paying back."

"Explain," Madison said.

"They mentioned *It*. My guess is whoever *It* is must owe the ugly bastards."

Madison took that in and mulled it over. "So Kim is the go-between and *It* is the lynchpin?"

"Possibly." I nodded and took a left. "Although, I don't think this is connected to the mission we're on."

"We won't know that unless we question Kim. I really

hope she's not a bad guy. I kind of like her for a human,"
Madison said as she laid her cheek on the passenger side
window.

"Are you okay?" I asked. My Mermaid looked a little
pale. It made my stomach do strange things. I didn't like the
feeling at all.

She smiled and punched me in the shoulder. "I'm good. I
just need to swim soon. I've been out of the water too long."

"In the ocean?" I asked, wondering how in the hell I
could get her to the ocean right now.

"No. That would be perfect, but it can be any kind of
water," she explained. "I'm fine for now. I'll find some water
after we figure out how our stage manager is involved. You
think she's gonna tell us who *It* is?"

"I do," I said glancing over at my gorgeous sidekick.
"The Gnomes might be scary, but together we're fucking
terrifying."

That's hot," Madison said with a wide smile

"I know. Right?"

We drove in silence—each of us lost in our own thoughts.
The area of town we were in was depressing. Tennessee was
actually a beautiful state, but not this part. Street after street
of run down homes and boarded up businesses. I was
surprised that Kim lived in an area like this with a child, but
maybe it was all she could afford which was total bullshit. If
Kim didn't turn out to be someone we would have to
eliminate, I was going to have a very fucking serious talk
with Dave about giving the woman a raise.

"We're almost there," Madison said.

"A few more blocks," I confirmed. And that's when I saw
it. My gut clenched and my sense of duty to my life choice

kicked in. It sickened me to think of the poor innocents trapped inside the craphole waiting for an unjust death. How in the fuck could I just drive by and not do anything?

Shitshitshit.

"Dang it," I muttered and wondered if I was about to make an incredibly stupid move.

I was.

With a loud screech of the tires, I whipped the car around and headed back the way we'd come.

"What are you doing?" Madison asked as I stopped the car in front of the shitty looking building.

"Can you give me ten minutes here?" I asked, glancing up and down the street to make sure I would be in the clear. It would suck all kinds of ass to get arrested by the human law enforcement.

"Umm... sure," Madison said, looking confused.

She was confused now. She was going to be either appalled or delighted in a few minutes.

"Get in the driver's seat. Keep the car running," I instructed as I cased the front of the building.

"What the heck are you about to do?" she asked, squinting at me.

I kissed the beautiful Mermaid on the lips. Hard. For all I knew after what she was about to witness, it might be the last time she would ever let me kiss her.

"I'm gonna do the right thing, Madison. I have to."

7

MADISON

As I sat in the idling car, I wondered if Rick was completely off his rocker. We had a mission to accomplish and he'd just made a pit stop at an animal shelter—and not a very nice one. It was seriously run down and awful looking.

Maybe he needed to be around other animals like I needed water. I didn't think that was a *thing* with Werewolves, but what did I know? Plus, if he needed to commune with other animals wouldn't it make more sense for him to seek out others of his own kind? Shelters were full of dogs and cats.

"Gods, if I didn't know he was a Vegan, I'd think he'd gone in for a quick snack—which would have been a deal breaker no matter how hot he is," I muttered to no one as I waited like instructed.

Sighing, I glanced up through the open sunroof. The stars twinkled in the cloudless night sky and a cool grass-scented summer breeze blew through the open windows. It made the depressing area look like it was bathed in a little magic.

Thinking back on the last hour, I grinned. Making out with the Werewolf was every kind of freakin' incredible. Keeping him was starting to sound really good. However, I was slightly concerned we would have hairy, fanged fish if we mated. I really needed to speak with my sisters about that terrifying prospect. As far as *dates* went this one was odd, but I had to give it a nine out of ten. It certainly wasn't boring.

The phone in my pocket buzzed and I glanced down at the caller ID. Shit. It was Poseidon. For a brief moment I considered letting it go to voice mail, but I wasn't irresponsible. I was violent and hazardous to my own health, but I was also a Mermaid warrior. Poseidon was my drunk general and I was part of his insane army at the moment.

"Hi, nard," I said as I answered.

"What did you call me?" the God of the Sea bellowed through the phone.

"Whoops, my bad. I thought you were someone else." I bit down on my lips to keep from laughing. Poseidon was such an easy target. And I knew he liked that I gave him shit. Other than his certifiable mate, Wally—Pirate Doug's mother—no one smack talked the drunk old fart like I did.

"Have you castrated Stew and peeled the skin off his heinous carcass yet?" he demanded.

"Umm... no."

"Then what in the Seven Seas have you been doing?" Poseidon shouted.

Pulling the phone away from my ear so I didn't go deaf, I rolled my eyes. "Trying to find the fucker," I snapped. "Plenty of Gnomes have been to see the show, but not Stew."

"*Have you found the Gnome Palace?*"

"Not yet, but Rick has an excellent plan. We're gonna to be human blenders and jump out of a plane tomorrow with the fixings for a smoothie—probably bananas, strawberries, yogurt and possibly some orange juice. Although, I think we should have some protein powder too since I'm not sure Rick gets enough protein in his diet. But powder might blow away in the wind. Anyhoo, if the parachutes hold, we should make it out in one piece. We can scope out the area from the air and find the Gnome Palace."

"*I didn't understand a gods' damned word of that,*" Poseidon admitted. "*However, I've been drinking since noon. Just find the bastard Gnome and level his arse. He's starting to send the lesser gods' body parts to me.*"

"Gross," I said with a gag. "Do you think they're dead?"

"*No. I would feel that. All the gods are connected and can feel when one is destroyed or in severe distress,*" he explained.

"That's kind of weird and awesome," I replied, impressed.

"*It sucks,*" he bellowed. "*Zeus has gastrointestinal issues regularly. We all fart like we've eaten a vat of fucking beans when that arse is on a toot bender.*"

I was speechless.

"*But not to worry. I occasionally chop off my own foot just to fuck with everyone—it grows back in an hour,*" he assured me.

I was more speechless.

"*Put Rick on the phone if he's still alive,*" Poseidon demanded.

"He's in an animal shelter," I told him, still flabbergasted at the wonky story I'd just heard.

"He got nabbed by animal control?" Poseidon asked, confused.

"Umm… no," I said, glad the idiot couldn't see my enormous eye roll. "He left me in the car to go into an animal shelter. Not sure why."

"For a quick snack?"

Poseidon surmised the same thing I had, which made me worry about my sanity if I was starting to think like the diaper wearing god.

"NO," I snapped, greatly relieved to be able to clarify that Rick wasn't a puppy murderer. "Rick is a Vegan. He doesn't eat animals."

"Right, my bad. I knew that," Poseidon recalled. *"Just find Stew and de-ball the bastard. The other gods are starting to imply that I don't deserve DIC."*

"You want Stew's dick?" I choked out.

If I'd known that detail, I never would have taken the job. However, I should have guessed. Poseidon did tell me to castrate the evil bastard. The God of the Sea sucked at sharing minor details. Delivering a Gnome wank was *not* a minor detail—at all. But if I hadn't taken the mission, I wouldn't have met Rick the Vegan nard who might be a keeper. Plus, I never would have known about zorbing.

Fine. If we had to deliver the Gnome King's dick to Poseidon, we would do it. Actually, Rick could do that part. I wasn't touching Stew's Johnson. Ever.

"Not dick. DIC," he shouted.

"Umm, that's about as clear as mud."

"Divine Immortal Circuit—not a pecker dick," Poseidon grunted with a chuckle. *"I do not want Stew's dick. When you*

castrate the arsehole, make him eat it. And after he does that, you can remove his epidermis and then behead him. Cool?"

"Umm… not really," I said with a gag. "How about we get the lesser gods back and you can deal with Stew."

Poseidon was silent for a long moment. I didn't know if that was a good thing or a bad thing.

"That sounds outstanding. I need some street cred back after all the shit I've taken for letting Stew kidnap the lesser gods on my watch. Just leave him in a cage and I'll take care of the rest."

"Will do," I said with a relieved sigh.

"However, you might have to end him if he plays dirty," Poseidon pointed out. *"And trust my drunk, diaper-wearing arse… the Gnomes play dirty."*

"Not a problem. I just don't want to lop his Johnson off."

"Yes, well, have fun and give my regards to Rick," he said and then hung up on me.

It was one of the strangest conversations I'd had with my *father figure* to date… and we'd had some weird ones.

"Put the car in gear," Rick shouted, barreling out of the shelter with at least ten dogs and equally as many cats following him.

"What the hey-hey?" I whispered, trying not to laugh. He was saving dogs and cats. My need to keep the dork was increasing by the moment.

"Get in, doggies and kitties," he huffed as he opened up the back of the SUV and began gently helping the menagerie into the vehicle. "Do not shit in my truck. I just had it cleaned and that will piss me off. You feel me?"

"I won't shit in your truck," I said with a giggle as an old and seriously underweight pit bull wiggled his way to the front of the pack and gave me a sloppy wet dog kiss.

"Oh my gods," Rick said quickly. "I didn't mean you, Madison. If you want to take a dump in my truck that's fine with me."

"Umm... thanks, but no. Not my thing," I said as a tiny kitten crawled into my lap and promptly fell asleep. "What exactly are we going to do with your new zoo?"

"Hang on," Rick yelled from the back of the truck as he made sure everyone was comfortable and then ran up to the passenger side door and got in. "Umm... so I..."

"Saved the doggies and kitties?" I supplied with a grin and a tilt of my head.

"Yes," he whispered, looking like a kid who'd done something really naughty. "I did. It's a high kill shelter."

"Mmmkay. Interesting side trip, but again... what are we going to do with all these animals?"

"You're not mad?" Rick asked, surprised.

"Why would I be mad?"

I was confused. I would have been pissed if he'd eaten them. I wasn't the least bit angry that he saved them. However, if he made this a habit, we would have to live on a fucking farm...

Wait. I was getting way ahead of myself here. *He* was going to have to live on a fucking farm. I lived on an island. Surprisingly, that thought depressed me.

"Most girls I know wouldn't be amused," he admitted with the beginnings of a smile pulling at his beautiful mouth.

"I'm not most girls."

"True," he said slowly as his smile became full.

The Werewolf's blue eyes sparkled and he was so

otherworldly beautiful, I found it difficult to breathe. I was so close to calling him a keeper, but we had a job to do first.

"Are we taking them back to the hotel?" I asked, changing the subject so I didn't suggest he bite me. "Might be kind of difficult to sneak this many animals in through the lobby. Maybe we could just make a giant sling with a sheet and tie them to us. We could scale the side of the building and take them in through the window to our suite. It's only on the tenth floor. We should be fine."

"Are you real?" Rick asked, staring at me strangely. "You would do that for my new friends and me?"

I wasn't sure how to answer. Did he think it was a stupid idea? I thought it was pretty creative and I adored scaling buildings.

"Umm… yes," I whispered, wondering if I was no longer a keeper in his mind because I was truly insane.

Next thing I knew I was in Rick's arms as he peppered little kisses all over my face. "PERFECT," he shouted with gusto. "You are fucking perfect."

A chorus of and barking and meowing backed up his delighted sentiment and I giggled as his kisses went from sweet to orgasm inducing.

"Gotta stop," I said as I ran my hands all over his broad chest and muscled shoulders. "We have company and we have to talk to Kim."

"Who's Kim?" Rick asked in a confused lustful daze.

"Dude," I said with a laugh as I regretfully pushed him away. "Kim—the stage manager who might be in cahoots with the Gnomes."

"Shit," he said running his hands through his thick blond

hair and gingerly adjusting the very hard junk in his jeans. "Right. Kim. Gnomes. Got it."

"You ready?" I inquired, still breathing heavily from our mini make out session.

"Born ready," he said with a lopsided grin. "We'll go question Kim and then we can bring the animals to my place in Kentucky. It's just an hour and a half away. Poseidon sent someone named Bonar to watch after the animals I already have."

"You're shitting me," I said with a laugh. "Bonar the Pirate?"

Rick's head jerked up and his eyes narrowed. "Yes. Do you know him?"

He was jealous. It would have been all kinds of sexy if it wasn't so laughable.

"Yep. I know him."

"And how well do you *know* him?" he demanded, going all Alpha wolf on me.

I couldn't hold back my burst of laughter. While I wanted to screw with him for being a jealous blowhard, I couldn't. I would hate it if he did that to me.

"Not biblically," I assured him as I touched the adorable dimple on his cheek. "Never biblically. He's a self-professed idiot arse. Bonar's like the profane, ancient Pirate brother I never wanted in my lifetime."

"Is he capable of protecting my animals?" Rick asked, clearly relived Bonar wasn't a past paramour of mine, but now concerned that he was too incompetent to take care of whatever kind of zoo Rick had amassed at his home.

"He's a Sphinx," I told him.

Rick's eyes went wide and he was stunned to silence for a moment.

"You're shitting me," he whispered.

"I shit you not."

"They still exist? I thought they were a myth."

"Yep. Bonar definitely exists. Your pets are very safe with him. I promise. He might be an arse, but he's a loyal and deadly arse," I told him.

"And the day keeps getting better," Rick said with a grin as he planted a kiss on my lips. "You ready to find out what Kim knows and who It is?"

"I was born ready," I said, repeating his earlier statement.

"That's what I like to hear."

And we were off—a car full of doggies and kitties with an insane Werewolf and a certifiable Mermaid running the show.

Life was getting very dangerous... and very good.

8

RICK

"HOLY SHEE-OT," I GASPED OUT AS QUIETLY AS I COULD.
"What the *fuck* am I looking at?"

We'd parked a block away from Kim's apartment
building, near a dog run. After letting the doggies and kitties
out for a quick whizz and a poopie, we'd put them safely
back in my truck and then quickly and quietly moved
through the shadows to Kim's residence.

My twenty new pets wanted to come on the adventure,
but even I knew that was a really bad plan. Madison
confirmed it before I could even suggest it. It was like she
could read my certifiably unstable mind which was pretty
awesome. She had already named the skinniest and frailest
of the dogs—it was an emaciated pit bull now known as
Thor. The dog was as besotted with the Mermaid as I was
and I didn't blame him a bit.

I hated leaving them since the furry little fuckers already
had abandonment issues. I knew what it was like not to be

wanted. I'd been ejected from my pack too many times to count over my three hundred years.

"What do you see?" Madison whispered as she hooked her combat boot-clad feet into the fire escape on the outside of the building and lowered herself down to the window. *"What the… What is that?"*

We were hanging upside down on the side of a four-story dilapidated brick apartment building. A fall wouldn't be a big deal. Four stories were a piece of cake. What really sucked was falling off of a twenty-story building. I could attest to that fact.

"Is it human?" I asked, squinting my eyes and pressing my face to the glass.

"Umm… I'm not sure," she said. "It's kind of cute in a seriously ugly way."

Kim was tearing around the studio apartment throwing clothing and toys into suitcases. The alien looking creature sat on the floor and calmly observed her sprint manically all over the room.

Kim sliced a mattress with a kitchen knife and pulled out a wad of money. She stuffed it into her pocket and then kissed the ugly thing on the top of his head.

"Guess she lied to the Gnomes about not having more money," I said as I watched her grab her laptop and phone and throw them into the open suitcase.

Kim paused only briefly as she glanced at a large framed poster from our cooking show—*Bitchin' in the Kitchen'*. She ran her hands over both my and Madison's faces and sighed with regret. "Best and most fun job I ever had," she said sadly and then got back to business.

"She likes being shouted at by Dave?" Madison asked,

confused.

"Actually, I think she might like *us*," I said, just as perplexed.

"Sweet Poseidon on a week long bender, I hope she's not evil," Madison muttered as she watched the scene inside the small apartment. "I like her. She breaks my heart."

"Ditto that."

Turning to the alien sitting on the floor, Kim squatted down and lovingly took its fugly face into her shaking hands. "Neville, we're going on a long, long, long vacation."

"Baycaytun!" the thing said with a drooly giggle.

"Gods, is that her child?" I asked, wondering what the hell the father could have looked like. "And she named him *Neville*? That kid is gonna take an ass-kicking on the playground all the way through college."

"If it is her kid, I hope Kim was wasted when she nailed the baby daddy," Madison mumbled.

As we hung upside down from the fire escape of the four-story building trying to figure out what the hell we were looking at, I realized I'd never been so happy in my life. The summer breeze caught Madison's pink curls and she looked like a princess even though all the blood had rushed to her head and made her face a bright pink.

"Do you like bunnies?" I whispered before I could stop myself.

"I've never had a bunny," she said, glancing over at me as we swung precariously from our perches. "Why?"

"Umm… no reason. Just curious."

"Mooomaid and Waaawuf," Neville shouted with glee as he pointed to the window we were hanging upside down in.

"Shit," I said as my eyes went wide and I pulled back

from the glass pane. "It's dark and we're wearing black. How did the alien see us?"

"Better question is how in the salty sea does he know what we are?" Madison said, pulling herself quickly up to the landing on the fire escape and yanking me with her.

Holy gods on fire but she was strong for a tiny thing. I was six foot three and two hundred and two pounds of pure muscle.

"I think it's time to go inside," I said. "Window or door?"

"Neither," Madison said with a grin. "Take my hand."

I did. I had no clue what she was about to do, but I was in. Any girl who could hang upside down off a building and send chocolate buttholes as a wedding present was a girl I could trust. Not that we wouldn't lose a limb or two along the way...

"Hang on tight," Madison said as her eyes sparkled with excitement. "I haven't done this in a while."

"Done what?" I asked, but it was too late.

In a blast of pink glitter she transported us right into Kim's tiny apartment. I was fairly sure my balls were now residing in my mouth and I couldn't exactly feel any of my appendages, but it was fucking fun—kind of like blowhole diving but with glitter.

"Oh my god," Kim shrieked as she went for a gun and stepped in front of her alien to protect him. "Are you working for them? I *knew* you weren't human."

"Put the gun down, Kim," Madison said, sternly. "It won't kill us."

"However, an extra hole in my head will seriously piss me off," I added, wiggling my fingers and toes to make sure they still functioned.

The alien peeked his bulbous head out from behind Kim's legs and grinned at me. His eyes were fucking enormous. It was somewhat terrifying, but Madison was correct. The thing was cute, in a seriously ugly way. His oversized head was covered in red hair that matched his mother's. I was fairly sure he had fangs, which was very strange indeed. However, the toddler's body was that of a normal sized human child albeit the arms and legs were a little short and squat.

"Waaawuf," Neville said pointing a stubby little finger at me with a giggle. "Grrrrrrrrr."

"What do you want?" Kim demanded, as she put the gun into her pocket and gently pushed the laughing alien behind her again. "I'm busy."

"Going somewhere?" I asked, glancing around the room and eyeing the overstuffed suitcases.

"I don't see how that's any of your business," she said, pulling a bottle of antacids from her pocket and shoving a handful into her mouth. "I'd like you to leave. Now."

Madison smiled and shook her head. "No can do, Kim. We have reason to believe you're in cahoots with the Gnomes."

"Are you freakin' serious?" she shouted as she pulled on her short hair and began to laugh hysterically.

It appeared that the woman was coming unhinged. The alien looked terrified and held on to her as she became more unwound by the second. Her laughter soon turned to a coughing fit and the poor human woman turned as red as the hair on her head.

"Umm... should I Heimlich her?" I asked, not quite sure how to proceed.

"Gods, I don't know," Madison said, looking unsure. "I think this might have been a bad idea."

"You think?" Kim yelled as her coughing fit subsided enough for her to speak. "I am *not* in cahoots with the Gnomes."

"Then why were you paying them?" I asked.

"You were *following* me?"

"Nope, we were given a lead on the Gnomes and you just *happened* to be there," I told her.

"Which does not bode well... for you," Madison added.

Kim glanced back and forth between Madison and me, trying to figure out if we were there to harm her or her alien. Since we weren't quite sure what the hell we were going to do, I was fairly sure she couldn't figure it out either.

"Look Kim," Madison said tightly. "Start talking now. We're after the Gnome King. If you're not on the side of the Gnomes, you need to convince me of that. Then you and your... umm..."

"Son," Kim said, beginning to calm down.

"Right. You and your son," Madison continued, "are free to go on vacation."

Kim was silent as she stared at us. We stared right back.

"So you're not really chefs?" Kim queried.

"Umm... no," Madison said with a chuckle.

Kim smiled weakly, but was still wary. "And you're not here to kill my son?"

Well, that certainly came from out of left field.

"Absolutely not," I huffed, wildly offended. "I'm Vegan Werewolf with an unhealthy penchant for death-defying hobbies. I *don't* kill children. Ever."

"What does being a Vegan have to do with anything?" Madison asked, squinting at me.

I had to think about that for a second. "Nothing," I admitted with a shrug. "I'm just not embarrassed about it anymore. I don't care who knows."

"Roger that," she said with a grin and then turned her attention back to Kim and the alien named Neville. "We are not here to kill anyone. We're trying to figure out why you were paying the Gnomes."

"You're going after the Gnome King?" she pressed, looking like an excited, nervous wreck.

Both Madison and I nodded.

"Why?" she asked.

"Classified," Madison shot right back. "And if you don't want to be taken into custody and sent to Mount Olympus to be questioned by a drunk assed god in a diaper then you'd better come clean now. Please."

"That was polite," I congratulated my Mermaid.

"Thank you," Madison replied. "There's no reason to be rude. Ever. My mom taught me that."

"My mom taught me that if I don't put the toilet seat down that I get my head flushed," I announced.

"How'd that work out?" Madison inquired, shaking her head and clearly trying not to laugh.

"I *never* leave the toilet seat up," I told her with a wink. "I train very well."

"Good to know," Madison said and then refocused on Kim.

"Would we be safe from the Gnomes on Mount Olympus?" Kim asked, sounding desperate.

What the hell was really going on here? No one in their

right mind would want to spend any time on Mount Olympus. The gods were fucking crazy.

Madison glanced over at me and I shrugged. We needed to get to the bottom of this fast or my new pets would eat the shit out of the interior of my truck.

"What do the Gnomes have on you?" I asked, Kim as her head dropped to her chest. "Why do they want to kill Neville other than that he's ug…" Before the entire word came out of my mouth, my Mermaid stabbed me in the ass with a wicked sharp dagger—and deservedly so. The alien couldn't help what he looked like. I was an ass of epic proportions to be rude to an innocent three-year-old.

"Thank you," I told Madison as I pulled the knife from my ass cheek, wiped off the blood and handed it back to her. My gal had my back.

"You're welcome," she replied, with her eyes still on Kim. "Answer Rick's question. Now."

"Neville is a half breed," Kim said softly, picking up the child and cuddling him close.

"Half what?" I asked, already knowing the answer.

Kim looked up at us with tears swimming in her eyes. "Half human, half Gnome."

"Holy hell and seashells, you had sex with a disgusting Gnome?" Madison blurted out and then handed me her dagger so I could return the favor.

I quickly and expertly stabbed her in her delectable ass. I had her back just like she had mine.

"Thank you," she said, removing the dagger and sliding it back into the holster.

"My pleasure," I replied.

Kim grabbed a piece of paper and a pen and began to

scribble out a note. Clearly, she didn't want her son to hear what she wanted to tell us. Handing the paper to me, she turned her back on us and gently rocked her sleepy child.

My gut clenched in fury as soon as I read the first line. Madison growled low in her throat.

And then we read.

Neville's father was violently murdered in front of me by the Gnomes — torn limb from limb and he never made a sound. He died as bravely as he lived.

And yes. He was a Gnome, but he wasn't like the others. I didn't know what he was when I met him and fell in love with him. He wasn't exactly good looking on the outside, but he was beautiful on the inside where it counts. We were only together a very short time, but it was good and right.

His death was his punishment for consorting with a human. After they killed him, I was beaten within an inch of my life and left for dead.

Somehow, by the grace of the gods, I survived the attack. However, I was left with something precious that would remind me of that night of horror for the rest of my life... and of the man I loved.

I went into hiding to protect my baby.

You might think I'm crazy, but while I was trying to decide what to do next, I had vivid dreams about a god. He was so real and familiar to me. He came to me every night for nine months and told me strange and wonderful stories about a little boy who would change the course of nature.

I received threats from the Gnomes when they caught wind of my situation, but for some unknown reason they never tried to kill me again.

I was terrified of what would happen to my son when he

arrived, but ending him was not an option for me. He was created in love. I wanted him.

And I'll never regret it.

Even before Neville entered this world, I fell madly in love with him. I would do anything for my child, and yes, I'm aware of what he looks like. He resembles his father and that is something to be proud of. His outsides aren't pretty but my baby's insides and heart are gorgeous and I thank the gods daily he's mine.

I will willingly die for Neville.

The Gnomes don't want anything to do with my child because of his heritage. He is less than nothing to them. However, they seem threatened by him at the same time.

They want money—money to let him live.

That's why I told you I couldn't get fired from my job. I need the money.

But the rules have changed and they want more. I don't have more except what I'd hidden for emergencies in my mattress. I've already sold everything I have of value and moved us into a home on the bad side of town.

I'm going to run. I'm hoping the Gnomes won't care enough to come after us. However, I think they will. I'm very aware that the gods are crazy. But if my child will be safe on Mount Olympus, I will happily scrub the floors of their palaces until my hands bleed. I can't stay here and risk Neville's life any longer.

Neville's father was named Dirk. He was the only son of the Gnome King—the very same bastard King that murdered him.

Holy freakin' shit. Kim had big balls. I respected women with big nards. Kim deserved better and I could make sure she got it.

The plan came to me quickly. It was slightly half-assed, but that was how I rolled. Madison was shaking with fury.

She moved to Kim and wrapped the trembling woman in a tight embrace. Neville laid his head on Madison's shoulder. It was beautiful.

My need to destroy the Gnome King wasn't beautiful. It was clawing at my gut like a disease. But first things first.

"Finish packing," I instructed as I began to throw more toys and clothes into the suitcases. "You're coming with us. I know of a place that you'll be safe. We're leaving in five so haul ass."

"Don't say *ass*. Neville is a baby," Madison chided me with a smile so wide I felt like a million bucks.

"My bad. You can stab me," I offered.

"No time," she said, helping me load the cases. "I'll stab you later."

"Good plan. Are either of you afraid of dogs or cats?" I inquired of a confused Kim and Neville.

"Umm... no," Kim said. "Are there dogs and cats on Mount Olympus?"

"Don't know," I replied. "We're not going there."

"Where are we going?" Kim asked, getting with the program and snapping the suitcases shut.

"We're going to Kentucky."

"Intukkeeee!" Neville shouted and clapped his hands.

"Safest place in the Universe at the moment," I promised as I scooped up the beautifully ugly alien and walked out the front door.

And it was. If there truly was a Sphinx at my house, no one could harm the alien.

Not even his soon to be dead grandfather.

"KIM, HOW DO I GET TO THE INTERSTATE FROM HERE?" I ASKED as I started my truck.

Madison sat shotgun and looked so pale it made my gut clench in terror. I could be blindfolded and drive a motorcycle off a cliff wearing nothing but my birthday suit and a parachute, but I couldn't stand Madison being ill. She'd fallen asleep the minute she'd settled herself in the car. We were an hour and a half from my place. I had three ponds, a whirlpool and a huge tub. She could have her pick. We just needed to get there. Fast.

The suitcases were strapped to the top of the vehicle, and there was just enough room for all twenty-four of us. Neville was thrilled with the furry menagerie and the feelings were mutual. They didn't give a shit what the boy looked like. The doggies and kitties all vied for a spot close to the little alien.

"Go six blocks south on Main Street," Kim said. "You'll pass a hardware store on your right and an aquarium on your left."

"Repeat," I said as I closed my eyes for the briefest second and grinned.

"Six blocks south on Main Street," Kim recited again.

"Not that part," I said, tersely.

"Hardware store on your right and aquarium on your left."

"Outstanding," I muttered and I slammed my foot down on the gas pedal. "That's what I thought you said."

There was no time to lose. Poseidon had been correct. My future *was* in Tennessee and she was sitting right next to me.

And I was damned sure I wasn't going to fuck up my future.

9

MADISON

THE DREAM WAS ABSOLUTELY DIVINE. SALTY WATER WASHED over my skin and a school of tiny orange fish tickled my scales. Screwing my eyes shut tight so I didn't wake up, I glided through the water and let it recharge my empty and tired soul.

Rolling and twisting, I laughed as the sting of the salt kissed me all over. My head cleared and the blood pumped through my veins with enchanted energy. Faster and faster I swam until my surroundings filled me up with what I was so desperately missing.

It was perfect... until I bashed my head into the glass wall. What in the farkin' Seven Seas was a *glass wall* doing in the ocean? Was Poseidon playing practical jokes again?

"Ouch," I shouted as my eyes popped open and I tried to get my bearings. Amazing dreams didn't usually end in black eyes and bruises.

"Mooomaid!" Neville shouted from the other side of the glass.

The little dude jumped up and down with rabid excitement as twenty dogs and cats joined him in his revelry. Kim stood next to her son and smiled and waved at me. My eyes quickly darted around the dry area and landed on the person I was pretty sure was responsible for this miracle.

With a thumbs up and a lopsided grin, Rick watched me swim with pride and awe. Quickly glancing down, I was grateful that my wild pink hair had been smart enough to remember to cover my girls. It wouldn't do to flash a three-year-old. My tail wiggled and sent me into a joyous backflip in the water. Snapping my fingers, a bejeweled blue bikini top appeared and covered my *assets*. It matched the gorgeous blue eyes of the crazy Werewolf who had found a closed aquarium for me to play in.

"Thank you," I mouthed to the man who I had every intention of keeping.

Rick nodded and approached the thick glass that separated us. Placing his hand on the glass, he waited. Without a second thought, I placed my hand opposite his and I could almost swear I felt his heat and desire. The simple action was far more intimate than our make-out sessions... and kind of wonderfully scary. Almost as terrifying as blowhole diving.

"Take as long as you need," he shouted through the glass with a wide grin. "Umm... can you breathe in there?"

I smiled and nodded. I could hold my breath for a week —longer if necessary. Mermaids were made for the water and our bizarre nature accommodated us to perfection. I knew we should be on the road, but five more minutes in the water would bring me back to full strength. Transporting Rick and myself into Kim's apartment had been a risky

move. I'd had no clue how much power that would take.
However, entrances were important and we'd made an
excellent one.

"Me swim with the Mooomaid," Neville said as he
waved his hands and magically transported to my side of
the glass.

"Holy shit," Rick shouted as his eyes went wide with
shock.

My expression matched Rick's. Neville was half human
and half Gnome. He was about to drown. The only calm
person in the aquarium was Kim—even the fish were
freaking out. She grabbed Rick and tried to hold him back as
he started to scale the enormous tank to retrieve the child.

What the heck was wrong with Kim? She told us she
would die for her child. I was going to stab her so hard in
the ass after Rick and I saved her son. I didn't give a salty
poop if she was human. My only worry was that Rick
wouldn't be quick enough.

With a massive flick of my powerful tail, I swam after the
wild child who was zipping around the tank like a freakin'
torpedo. How in the ever-lovin' Seven Seas was Neville that
fast? I was a speed demon and could barely keep up.

"He's fine," I heard Kim yell as she banged on the glass.
"He can hold his breath for hours."

Well, that was certainly interesting. How in the heck was
that possible?

Rick looked doubtful as he slowly climbed back down
and watched as Neville sped around the tank like he'd
ingested a vat of espresso laced with speed.

"Dude," I hissed, grabbing the little sucker as he zipped
by. "What the heck is going on here?"

Neville babbled under the water a mile a minute. I couldn't make out a word of his excited gibberish. However, I was flabbergasted that he could speak underwater like I could.

"Five minutes are up, little dude," I said, holding the wiggling anomaly against my chest as I swam to the top of the huge tank and looked for a ladder to get out.

Rick was waiting for us still looking shell-shocked.

"I think I might have lost a century of my life watching that," he said with a wince.

"Kim's *not* completely human," I grumbled as I passed him a soaking wet and very happy Neville.

"Ya think?" Rick said with a chuckle. "Our stage manager has been holding out on us."

"The truth shall set you free," I said as I sadly let my tail morph back to legs. "I hope for Kim's sake she wants to be free. Or she's gonna have a knife scar in her butt like nobody's business."

"I'M COMPLETELY *HUMAN*. I SWEAR," KIM INSISTED FOR THE umpteenth time as Rick drove like a racecar driver with a death wish to his Kentucky home.

The ride was awesome. Kim's answers were not.

"That's *not* possible," I told her. "Gnomes can't even swim. There is no way in Poseidon's salty oceans that Neville should be able to swim, much less talk under water."

"What did the little alien dude say?" Rick asked as he made a screeching sharp left turn onto a gravel road in the middle of nowhere.

"Umm… I couldn't tell you—didn't understand a word," I replied as I glanced back in frustration at the soundly sleeping Neville cuddled in his mother's arms. "What else can he do?"

"There are new things daily," Kim admitted hesitantly, holding on to her child and the seat of the careening car for dear life.

"Spit it out, Kim," Rick said. "I'm not sure how, but I'm beginning to think you being our *stage manager* was not an accident."

Glancing sharply over at Rick, I marveled that someone who had landed on his head as many times as he had in his life was so brilliant.

"You think I set this up?" Kim asked, aghast.

"Nope," I answered for Rick as he looked over at me and raised a brow. "I think someone else might have."

"Who?" Kim asked, terrified. "The Gnomes?"

I shook my head and sighed. "No, someone who wants the Gnome King dead. But I can't figure out the connection."

"Neither can I," Rick said. "And apropos of nothing, my house is kind of messy."

"Define *kind of*?" I asked with a laugh and an eye roll.

"Shit show of epic proportions, but the toilet seats are down," he replied sheepishly as he pulled up to a cozy looking log cabin bathed in bright moonlight. He stared at it in shock with his mouth agape.

I wasn't real sure what Rick considered messy, but it looked freakin' spotless by my standards. "What's wrong?" I asked.

"I have grass," he whispered.

"You have gas?" I asked, with a wince. "That's TMI, dude."

"No. *Grass*," he said, completely perplexed. "And it's been mowed. And there are no broken windows. There should be four blown up car carcasses in the front yard. And the steps leading up to the front porch are supposed to have a big burn hole in them from the time I accidentally set them on fire when I tried to blow up the vacuum cleaner that shredded the shit out of my favorite boxer briefs."

While I was secretly delighted he wore boxer briefs instead of tighty whities, I wondered if he'd taken a wrong turn somewhere along the way. It was after three in the morning.

"Umm… is this even your house?" I asked.

"It looks like my house, but better," he said, bewildered.

And that was when it went from weird to weirder. Well, not for me, but definitely for Rick.

"Avast ye, and show yerself, ye peg-legged salty sea nard of a bandana wearing pontoon splinter," a very familiar voice bellowed from somewhere in the darkness. "If yarr has come for the critters, ye'll be beggin' to be a greasy haired rope burn in Davy Jones' locker."

"What the hell was that?" Rick snarled looking around the yard in a panic. "You guys stay in the car. I'm gonna go kill it. It sounds mentally deranged."

"No can do," I said with a laugh as I got out of the car much to Rick's dismay. "It will just rise from the ashes as a baby and you'll have to raise it. Trust me on this. I've seen it happen."

Rick was out of the car in a flash and shoved me behind

him. His fangs had dropped, his claws were out and his eyes glowed a bright eerie silver.

It was freakin' hot.

"Bonar, you nard. Show yourself. It's me, Madison," I yelled into the night.

"Madison," Bonar bellowed with delight as he appeared in front of us followed by what I could only call a herd of bunnies, deer, and raccoons. "And who's the cod faced tar stain standin' in front of ye?"

"It's Rick. The owner of the zoo you're protecting."

The air was thick with testosterone and I rolled my eyes. Bonar eyed the Werewolf and Rick eyed the dumbarse Pirate Sphinx. I smiled and shook my head realizing how bizarre my friend must appear to Rick. Bonar was wearing his typical breeches, knee-high boots and puffy shirt. Strangely, the hairy little Pirate was cute… in a shriveled up, pruney kind of way. After the men glared like idiots and sized each other up for one minute and thirty-two seconds, both grinned and shook hands.

"Yar a shite housekeeper, Rick. Took me a week to batten down the hatches on yer crab infested shite hole of a land farin' abode. It's a right man o'war now."

"I have crabs?" Rick asked, confused.

"You'd better not," I muttered with another eye roll.

"Nay, ye eyeliner wearing dingy dangler," Bonar grunted, picking up a raccoon and scratching its head with affection. "Yer a slob."

"Oh," Rick said with a relieved nod of understanding. "I already knew that."

"So are ye done with yer cookin' show? Did ye castrate the stripey sweatered son of a sea snake Gnome King and skin the bastard alive?" Bonar inquired as if that was a normal activity to take part in.

"Holy shit, are we supposed to do that?" Rick asked me with a slight gag.

"No," I assured him with a shudder. "We're just supposed to leave the jackhole in a cage and return the lesser gods to Mount Olympus. Poseidon will de-pecker the abomination."

Bonar and the zoo wandered over to the car and peeked in. "Looks like ye added to yar pack," he said with a chuckle as the dogs began to bark and the cats mewed. "And who might the lovely lassie and handsome wee bairn be hidin' there amongst the doggies and kitties?"

"Did he say *handsome*?" Rick whispered to me in horror.

I nodded, unable to speak. Was Bonar blind? I mean, Kim was adorable, but Neville? Neville was *not* adorable. At all. He was sweet, but umm… unfortunate looking.

Bonar puffed out his chest, spit on his hand and then swiped it through his gnarly hair to impress the *lassie*. At least that's what I thought he was doing.

"I'm Kim, and this is my son, Neville," Kim said as she got out of the car and blushed so red I thought she might pass out. "It's a pleasure to meet you."

"Aye, the pleasure is all mine I assure ye," Bonar said, bowing low to Kim.

It looked more like he was squatting to take a dump than pay his respects, but Kim clearly didn't notice if her girly giggle was anything to go by.

"What the hell is happening here?" Rick hissed in my ear. "I'm so fucking confused."

"I think Bonar is hitting on Kim," I said under my breath. "This could get nightmare inducing."

"I'm on it," Rick said, sprinting over to the car before Bonar professed his undying love. "Excuse me, Boner."

"It's Bonar," I corrected him with a giggle.

"Right. My bad. Bonar," he amended and just kept right on going, ignoring the fact that he'd just called a deadly Sphinx Pirate an erection. "Kim and her alien son, Neville need protection from the Gnome fuckers. I busted the doggies and kitties out of a high kill shelter earlier this evening. It's against my life choice as a Vegan to let innocent animals die. Therefore, I'm now responsible for them. Madison and I have to go back to Tennessee in the morning to be human blenders so we can suss out the location of the Gnome Palace and cage the King so Poseidon can rip his pecker off at some point."

Bonar simply nodded his head and appeared wildly confused. I didn't blame him. I was a little confused too and Rick wasn't done yet.

"Neville is half Gnome and half human which I call bullshit on since the wild little bastard can swim and talk under water. Kim won't give up what she really is, but she has huge nards and we like her... *as you clearly do as well*... so she can live. What we need is for you to guard over Kim, Neville, and the shit load of animals I've recently acquired along with the zoo I've already amassed until the Gnome prick is taken care of. Cool?"

Thankfully, Neville was fast asleep and heard none of the shitty language Rick had just spewed. That saved him from a double stabbing later.

"Aye, methinks so," Bonar said with a nod. "Lovely Kim,

may I be so bold as to ask ye a personal query?"

"Of course," Kim said with another giggle.

Bonar cleared his throat three times and pulled his sagging breeches up so high that I was certain he'd just given himself a permanent wedgie. Rick moaned in phantom pain as Bonar's buttcrack was now clearly defined by his breeches.

"Gods, that has to hurt," Rick whispered.

"Shhh," I whispered back, trying not to laugh. "I just hope he doesn't turn around. The view from the front has to be terrifying."

Bonar again cleared this throat. "Beautiful Kim, are ye involved with a scallywag at the moment?"

"Umm... no," Kim said, blushing furiously. "I'm not. Are you?"

Bonar blushed a deeper red than Kim. It was horrifyingly charming in a gross kind of way. Clearly looks weren't high on Kim's agenda for a man.

"Can't say as I am," Bonar replied with the widest grin I'd ever seen on his face. "Would ye like to see the cabin? We can tuck the handsome wee bairn in and then might I tempt ye with a jigger of rum and a moonlight spin around the property with the raccoons?"

"I would like that very much," Kim said. "You are quite the gentleman."

My sisters were never going to believe this. I had half a mind to take out my phone and record it. However, I would never do that to the Pirate. Bonar was an arse, but he was also kind and good. He did have sticky fingers and love of stealing from Target, but he was a sweet and truly loyal immortal badass weirdo.

"Come now, lassie," Bonar said, gently taking the sleeping Neville from her and placing Kim's hand in the crook of his arm. "Ye don't have to worry yer pretty head no more. Bonar will take care of ye and the handsome wee bairn."

As they walked into the house, Rick and I stood in stupefied silence.

"Are they going to bang in my guest room?" Rick choked out in a horrified whisper.

I shrugged and laughed. "Don't know and don't want to know," I said. "But there is something I'd like to see while we're here."

"What's that, Mermaid?" he asked, still trying to recover from the visual he'd clearly conjured up in his mind.

"I'd like to see your bedroom," I told him as I felt my body tingle with excitement and a little fear.

"Are you sure?" he asked, beginning to grin. "Once you enter the man cave, you're mine."

I looked up at the beautiful man who was equally as nutty as I was and I sighed with happiness. "Rick, I think I would like to keep you."

"Madison, I *know* I would like to keep you. Knew it from the moment I saw you."

Inhaling in through my nose and blowing the air slowly out of my mouth, I mentally prepared to throw myself into the deep end of the ocean. Nothing had ever seemed so right. "Take me to the man cave, Rick."

"Hell. To. The. Yes," he shouted as he threw me over his shoulder and sprinted so fast I got dizzy.

The man was insane.

And the man was mine.

MADISON

GLANCING OVER AT THE GREEK GOD CLAD ONLY IN TIGHT GRAY boxer briefs, I giggled. The gods broke the mold after they made him—and a good thing too. The immortal world couldn't handle two of him. Hell, I wasn't sure I could handle one of him.

"Can't think when all the blood from my brain goes to my Johnson," Rick said, cupping my breasts in his hands and giving me a sexy smirk that sent my lower regions into overdrive. "Should we talk first before we boink? I want to do this right, Madison. We only get one first time."

It was so sweet, I wanted to cry. This decision was right. However, I was going to make the talk very *hard* for him—pun completely intended.

"What do you want to talk about?" I asked, untying my sarong and letting it fall to the floor in his very tidy man cave.

Rick had shrieked like he was being chased by Hades when we'd entered his bedroom—scared the scales out of me. Clearly, he didn't recognize it cleaned up. Bonar had been seriously busy. After checking a few drawers for explosives and the closet for his sky diving gear, he calmed down and realized we were indeed in his man cave.

"What's your favorite color?" he asked, with a whistle of appreciation for my hot pink thong.

"Pink," I said automatically. "Yours?"

"Definitely pink," he said, grabbing the bedpost of his huge bed to keep from launching himself at me before we were finished with our *talk*. "Libation?"

"Piña colada," I said with a laugh. "You?"

"Piña colada," he replied without hesitation.

"Duuuude, you don't seem like a piña colada kind of Werewolf. You can't just repeat my answers back to me," I told him, easing my barely-there thong down my legs as his eyes grew wide with desire.

"Fine," he said with a sheepish grin. "It used to be beer, but I changed my mind because you make a piña colada sound so dang hot. You ask the next question so I can't copy you."

"Okay," I said, unhooking my jeweled bikini top and tossing it across the room. "This is good. We need to know the little things about each other before boinking for keeps."

"Right," Rick wheezed out as his eyes pinned themselves to my girls.

With a naughty grin, I ran my hands down my body and perched myself seductively on the edge of his enormous bed. "Favorite restaurant?"

"Hooters," he blurted out, in a haze of lust.

"Oh my gods. Seriously?" I demanded with a laugh.

"Wait." He slapped himself in the head. "What was the question again?"

"Forget it," I said, laying back on the bed and arching my back so the view was positively carnal. "Let's try another. Favorite movie?"

Rick began to pace the room in a sweat. His eyes were still glued right where I wanted them—on me.

"Movie," he muttered as he slammed into his dresser and barely noticed. "Movie. Favorite movie. I can do this… I'd have to say my favorite movie is Naked Knockers and Hot Ass on my Bed. SHIT." He froze in mortification, grabbed my dagger and stabbed himself in the butt. "I didn't mean that. I mean, *I did*, but that's not a movie as far as I'm aware. My favorite movie is *Splash*."

Jerking up to a sitting position, I stared at him with my mouth agape. "For real?"

"For real." He moved toward the bed, stalking me like prey.

Gone was the bumbling boy. The sexy man had arrived. Seashells in a sandstorm, it was the hottest thing I'd ever seen.

"That's *my* favorite movie," I told him, feeling my excitement ramp up to danger zone.

"You copying *me* now?" he asked as he sprinted the last few feet and jumped onto the bed causing both of us to bounce like popcorn.

"Guess so, dummy," I told him as I rolled him to his back and straddled him. "Are we done with question time?"

"Yessss," he hissed through clenched teeth as I wiggled on top of him. "I really don't want to have to stab myself again. It's way more fun when you do it."

"Have you ever hung upside down from a chandelier and boinked?" I whispered in his ear as I ran my hands over his gorgeous body. I wasn't even sure if it was possible, but it sounded hot and dangerous. The chance of electrocution was high.

"No, but I'm up for it," he said with a chuckle as he ran his tongue over my collar bone and then repeated the motion with his razor sharp and *oh so sexy* fangs. "Only problem is I don't seem to have a chandelier handy."

"Not a problem," I told him as I raised my hands high.

With a clap and a wish, an enormous glittering pick chandelier with thick, flat crystal arms appeared on the ceiling. However, just in case the adventure went awry, I made the lighting fixture out of plexiglass. It would suck to end up losing an arm due to shards of glass. I also anchored it well, I really didn't want either of us to break our necks mid-boink. We would most likely snap them tomorrow when we jumped from the plane. Tonight was all about pleasure. Well, tomorrow was too, but a different kind.

"Niiiice," Rick said as he grabbed my hands and yanked me to a standing position.

Quickly stripping bare, he glanced at me with a lopsided smile and flexed his muscles. He was so beautiful I almost couldn't catch my breath. But more important than his exquisite outsides were his certifiably insane and beautiful insides. The thought of spending eternity waking up to a man who wanted to take me zorbing filled my tummy with joyful tingles.

"Wait," I said, as he started to jump on the bed in preparation to take a flying leap up to the lighting fixture we were about to defile. "I need to say something."

Rick stopped jumping which was kind of sad because it was so hot, but that was my own fault. Gently laying me down on the bed, he lay next to me. He pressed his forehead to mine and held me. It was the simplest of moves, but I felt so safe and happy in his strong arms.

Pressing my lips to his, I sighed. I needed to tell him what was in my nutball head. I wanted him to know so he had time to back out.

"Umm... I want to keep you forever," I whispered, screwing my eyes shut so I had the nards to finish what I needed to say. "If we boink—which I *really* want to do—you need to know I'll slice your Johnson off with a dull butter knife if you ever stray."

"Sounds reasonable," he said, against my mouth. "What else?"

So far so good. "Do you have any clue what we would have if we got pregnant?"

"Pretty sure we'd have a baby," he said, nibbling on my neck.

"No... I mean, will it be a hairy fish with claws and fangs?" I asked, tangling my hands in his thick blond hair.

He looked up and me and laughed. "If it is, it will be the most beautiful hairy fish with claws and fangs in the Universe. I will love it more than anything in the world because it's ours."

I was stunned to silence. He was right. I would love our baby too, no matter what the little daredevil looked like. Love was blind. I now understood why Bonar saw a handsome wee little bairn in Kim's arms. Kim's devoted love to Neville made him beautiful.

Rick cupped my face and ran his thumb over my lips. "Can I add something here?"

His touch warmed me all over. His nearness made my heart beat faster. "Yes," I whispered.

"I'm in love with you, Madison. I've never really belonged anywhere until I met you. No one has ever understood me or taken the time to really care until you," he said, gently tucking some of my wild pink curls behind my ear. "All my pack ever saw in me was the insane dude with the death wish that they didn't want around. You see me. You see me clearly. And you still want to keep me."

"And you see me," I told him, wrapping my arms around him and hugging him tight. "You see more than the violent pink haired Mermaid who likes to blow shit up and bungee jump naked."

"Naked?" he asked, wildly impressed.

"Totally," I promised with a giggle. "You'll have to try it sometime."

"I'm in, baby. I'm all in."

"I love you, Werewolf," I said as my rose-colored eyes filled with happy tears. "I will always see you and always love you no matter what."

"Come with me," Rick insisted as he stood up, held me close and took a giant leap off the bed.

Thanks to his lupine strength, we were now perched precariously on the shimmering chandelier. My body was aligned with his and felt molten as I started to come apart in his arms. Not to mention his very impressive Johnson pressed against my stomach might have had something to do with it...

"Mine," Rick hissed as he flipped me upside down and

hooked my legs over one of the chandelier arms. He hung on with one hand and kept me where he wanted me with the other. It was freakin' fantastic. All the blood rushing to my head made me a bit dizzy, but Rick was completely responsible for making me almost pass out in ecstasy. His talented mouth and fangs went to work and I couldn't have uttered my name if my life depended on it.

"Sweet chicken of the sea in a tube top," I screamed as a strong orgasm ripped through me causing crystals on the chandelier to explode.

"You liked that?" Rick asked, oozing with masculine pride as he flipped me back over and wrapped my legs around his waist. "Not sure what the actual physics of what we're about to do are, but I'm gonna give it a go. You in?"

"Forever," I said, reaching down to greet his very excited Johnson.

"Gods," he said, letting his head fall back on his shoulders. "I'll give you the rest of my immortal life to never stop doing that."

"Deal," I replied with a giggle as I got to *know* him better.

As we attempted to arrange ourselves into a position that would work, we laughed like little kids doing something very naughty. It was like Twister on crack and it rocked.

"Holy shit," Rick shouted and laughed as the ceiling began to cave in.

We'd gotten way too hot and heavy waaaay too fast. With an explosive *pop* the chandelier fell from the ceiling with a huge crash and all the electricity in the house went out.

"Whoops," I said with a giggle as I crawled out from underneath the huge broken mess. I silently congratulated myself that the chandelier was not made of glass. "My bad. I thought I anchored it better."

"As long as you're still good to boink, I don't care if you blow up the entire house. Except maybe not the guest rooms. I'd feel really bad if Neville had to grow a new appendage. He's just a little dude."

"Roger that," I said as I removed the debris with a wave of my hands and hopped onto his king-sized bed. "Take two?"

"And three and four and five and six and seven…"

I rolled my eyes and smiled. "You can go that many times?"

"I'm a Werewolf, baby. I can go all night."

We wasted no time getting down to business. As we became one, we both cried out at the incredible feeling. It was more intense and perfect than blowhole diving. Loving someone elevated sex to a level I was unaware existed. Orgasms numbers two, three and four overtook me and I screamed with delight. My body trembled and I clenched him inside me as I rode out the aftershocks.

"You still with me?" Rick asked as he cradled my face in his hands and kissed me until my toes curled.

"Always," I whispered as my body again arched toward his.

The Werewolf was a freakin' sex maniac—and I loved it. As soon as the fifth orgasm ended another consumed my body.

"I love you, Madison, you certifiably crazy woman," he said, still inside me.

"I love you more, Rick you batshit nutty freak of nature."

"Perfect," he said with a wide grin as he began to torture me with his expertise again.

I kept my rose-colored eyes glued to his brilliant blue. The need and savage lust I saw there made my heart and body sing. Rick was not a man. He was an animal—*my* animal. His desire for me matched mine for him and it was positively explosive in the best way possible.

"Round seven?" Rick inquired politely as his lips found my girls and made colorful sparkles pop behind my eyeballs.

"I'll take round seven and then demand a round eight," I said as I gasped for air.

"Deal."

The speed of our lovemaking increased and Rick grew wild like the sexy beast he was. I writhed like a Mermaid in heat beneath him and we headed toward a massive orgasm together that was probably going to ensure that Bonar would have to rebuild part of the cabin tomorrow.

Rick's grin and all the naughty sexy things he whispered in my ear sent me right over the edge into number seven.

"I love you," he shouted as he came.

And I loved him. I would love him forever.

He was a total keeper.

11

MADISON

"Well, me bucko," Bonar said to Rick as he served up a breakfast of oatmeal with apples, almonds and cinnamon, mixed berries, avocado toast with flax seed and chia seed on it, vanilla rice milk and fresh squeezed orange juice. "Methinks yer plan has some scurvy holes in it."

"This is fucking delicious," Rick shouted, shoving three pieces of avocado toast into his mouth at the same time. "And I agree with you about the plan. But since we don't know where the Gnome Palace is, it's the best we can do. Anyhoo, I've never been a human blender before and the thought of jumping out of a plane while making a smoothie with the sexiest Mermaid alive is damn hot."

"Agree," I said with a giggle. "The worst that can happen is we break a few bones if the chutes don't open. I can heal from a busted femur in an hour. And from the air we can suss out the location of the Palace."

"My girl is a freak of nature," Rick announced with pride. "And she looks amazing naked."

That's when I stabbed his hand to the table with a fork. There was a three-year-old present. Not to mention Bonar and Kim. Rick had a TMI problem.

"Thank you, babe," Rick said with a rueful grin. "I keep forgetting Neville is just a little alien dude."

"No worries," I said with a smile as I yanked the fork out of his hand. "That's why I'm here."

"So ye stab the thunderin' bilge rat when he misbehaves?" Bonar asked, with a raised brow.

"I do," I told him a little defensively. I knew our habits were a little odd, but they worked for us. "Usually in the butt. Since he's sitting down and I don't have a knife, I improvised. He stabs me too."

"I do," Rick confirmed proudly. "We have each other's backs."

"Tis alarmingly interesting," Bonar said with a knowing smirk. "T'will there be another weddin' in the future?"

Rick looked over at me and grinned so wide I did something stupid. Something I said I would never do after attending my sister's recent shit show of a wedding.

"Umm... possibly."

"Definitely," Rick corrected me. "Definitely a wedding with a Vegan wedding cake shaped like a blowhole."

"Blowhole," Neville shouted with delight.

"That's right, buddy," Rick said, giving the little guy a high five. "Someday when you're old enough, I'll take you blowhole diving in Hawaii."

"Yayayayayayayayay!" Neville squealed.

"Shit," Kim mumbled under her breath.

"Just know that I'm makin' meself available to officiate yer nuptials," Bonar offered.

"Will you call me a swimming hooker during the vows?" I asked, narrowing my eyes at the Pirate.

"Nay," he said quickly with his hands held high in surrender. "Learned me lesson with yer sister 'bout that. Still have a scar on me arse for that blunder."

"Well, then... okay," I said and then immediately wanted to take it back. But Bonar seemed so delighted and honored I didn't have the heart. Maybe he could make up for the debacle of Tallulah's wedding by performing mine. Or maybe not...

Deciding to ignore my epic mistake of saying yes to the wedding officiating mess, I dug into my oatmeal and then paused. Holy hell and seashells, there were no animal products anywhere on the table. My adoration for the gnarly, sweet, idiot Pirate grew even more.

"Bonar, thank you. This breakfast awesome," I told him with a grin and a wink.

"Tis nothing, me little Mermaid," he said with a jaunty bow. "Methinks to go Vegan too. Bein' with the critters has got me to thinkin'."

"Neville doesn't like meat at all," Kim said as she helped Bonar serve the meal like they were a well-oiled and natural team of two. "And forget about seafood," she added with a laugh, patting her little man on the head and kissing his chubby toddler cheek. "Last time we were in the grocery store, he magically stole all the live crabs when my back was turned, brought them home and set them up in our tub. I didn't even realize he'd done it till I went to run his bath that night."

Dropping my spoon, I stared at Neville in surprise. I was stunned. Not because of what the little dude had done, but because I'd done the same thing so many times in my life I couldn't even count them.

"What about pet stores?" I asked, still watching Neville who was now peering over at me with an adorably naughty grin.

He really was kind of cute...

Kim let her head fall to the table with a thud. "We do *not* go in pet stores," she said. "Especially the fish aisle."

"Why?" I demanded, feeling kind of tingly. "Why not the fish isle?"

"Do you want to tell them or should I?" Kim asked Neville.

"Me tell," he shouted with a belly laugh. "Fish no like it there. So me clapped me hands and me send them home."

"Home?" I pressed, growing lightheaded. Could Kim possibly have Mermaid blood in her? All of Neville's actions led me to believe she might.

"The saltwater fish he sent back to the ocean... or so he told me, and all of the freshwater fish ended up in local ponds all over the area," Kim finished the story for her little boy.

"How did ye find out?" Bonar asked with interest, while also focusing on Neville.

"It was on the evening news," Kim said with a shake of her head and a chuckle. "All of the local ponds had many newly acquired occupants. No one knew how they got there except Neville and me. Hence, no more visits to the pet store."

"Kim," I said as casually as I could. "Tell me about your parents. Do they live nearby?"

Kim's eyes lit up, but her smile was melancholy. "They

had me very, very late in life. They both died long before Neville was born. It's one of my greatest sorrows that my parents didn't know their grandson."

Rick was catching on quick as was Bonar if the expressions on their faces were anything to go by. It didn't bode well for my hypothesis that Kim's parents had died— or that they lived in a landlocked area, but something was off here and I knew I was onto something. Rick was of no help. His mouth was full of so much food, I wasn't sure how he was going to swallow it without choking. I really needed to have my head examined because I even thought his iffy table manners were hot. Bonar was a very patient Pirate and simply observed. That left the questioning up to me.

"Umm… do you have any idea how old they were when they died?" I asked searching for a clue that might prove me right.

"Actually I don't," she said with a shake of her head. "Never found their birth certificates or driver's licenses. They never seemed to age though. Well, not until the end when we relocated to Tennessee. I grew up on the coast of Florida."

I was tingling all over now. Mer-people in landlocked areas would eventually wither away and die. But why would they choose to die? "And why did you move to Tennessee?"

"My father said our future was in Tennessee. Weird, but that's what he said," she replied with a wistful sigh and a small smile. "Ironically, he was right. Neville is my future and I never would have had him if I hadn't moved to Tennessee. My future is… well, *was* in Tennessee."

Kim glanced shyly over at Bonar who was grinning like

he'd won the lottery. And maybe he had. Kim and her son were pretty awesome even if I still had no clue what they really were. Bonar might not be the snappiest dresser, or the sharpest tool in the shed, but he was every kind of truly beautiful—especially on the inside where it counted most. Of course, their courtship *was* kind of fast, but sometimes—if you were really lucky—you knew you'd met your true love immediately.

"The soused, diaper-wearing buttdong told me my future was in Tennessee," Rick said as he miraculously swallowed the ridiculous amount of avocado toast that he'd shoved into his mouth. "Those were his exact words. And I have to admit the drunken bastard was correct."

Rick took my hand and kissed it. Keeping him was the best plan I'd ever had.

"So the diaper wearing buttdong got it right?" I asked, turning his hand over and kissing the spot where I'd stabbed him.

"Yep, the diaper wearing buttdong hit the nail on the head," he replied with a wide grin.

I laughed. I'd have to remember that one to tell my sisters. I couldn't wait to see the expression on Poseidon's face when I called him a *diaper wearing buttdong*.

"Soooo," Bonar said, bringing Kim a plate of food and sitting down beside her. "Do ye think it's possible that yer folks might have been really old?"

"Define really old," Kim said, perplexed.

"Over two hundred?" I volunteered.

Kim exploded into laughter. "That's not possible."

"I'm three hundred," I pointed out.

"Same here," Rick added.

"I'm three thousand," Bonar said as Kim paled considerably.

"I keep forgetting you people are immortal," she whispered and then closed her eyes. "Neville is probably immortal too."

"Okay," I said, trying to put a very large puzzle together in my head by figuring out the missing pieces. "I know it's rude to ask a human woman her age… but how old are you, Kim?"

Kim appeared to be shocked and distraught for a moment and then started to cry. Shit. If I'd known she was so sensitive about her age, I wouldn't have asked. Humans were freakin' touchy. And I really didn't see the problem. Kim didn't look a day over thirty.

"I'm sorry," I said. "You don't have to answer."

"Actually, I do," she said, sniffling and wrinkling her brow in worry. "You see, I have some kind of horrible genetic disorder. I stopped going to the doctor years ago because of all the invasive questioning and doubt."

"Spit it out, woman," Rick said, digging into a huge bowl of oatmeal. "You can't be over thirty."

"I'm sixty-five," she mumbled.

"What the fuck?" I shouted. "Get out of town. There is no motherhumpin' ball eating way in the Seven fucking Seas that you're sixty-five."

Rick grabbed the knife, held it up, and cocked his head toward Neville who had clearly heard and understood my inappropriate rant. Standing up and turning around so Rick had access to my butt, I nodded my head.

Quickly and expertly, he stabbed me in the ass. I was so lucky to have him.

"Thank you," I said, sitting back down. "I'd like to apologize for my potty mouth. I'm not used to being around children. However, Kim… if you're truly sixty-five, you are *not* all human."

"It's a disease," she insisted, looking a little bewildered.

"Who told you it was a disease?" I asked. Did her parents screw with her head?

"No one. I figured it out myself," she shouted as she stood up and accidentally knocked her plate to the floor. "I'm so sorry," she muttered in tears as she went to clean it up.

"Nay, me darlin'," Bonar said, softly as he gently pushed her out of the way and took care of the mess. "Just sit yerself back down by yer boy. I've got this."

Kim did as she was told. Her hands were shaking and her eyes had grown wild. "If I was something other than human, why didn't my parents tell me so?" she demanded, looking at all of us for an answer we couldn't give her. "I've spent most of my life worrying I would die tomorrow since I had this disorder."

She was crying harder now and both of the men in her life—Neville and Bonar—put their arms around her to comfort her.

Looking over at Rick, I picked up the knife and handed it to him, but he wouldn't stab me.

"You haven't done or said anything wrong," Rick said, putting the weapon back down in the table.

"Then why do I feel so awful?" I asked.

"Because you're compassionate," he replied with a smile that made my heart feel light. "It's one of the things I love about you, along with your passion for blowhole diving and your fabulous knockers."

My Werewolf certainly had a *way with words*, but it was the thought that counted most.

"Thank you," I said, feeling a little better.

"You're my dream come true," he said and planted a kiss on my nose.

Wait. Wait a farking minute. Dream... *Dream*. Dream come true?

"KIM," I shouted, startling everyone including myself. "Your dream."

"What dream?" she asked, wiping her tears with a hanky that Bonar had conjured up for her.

"When you were pregnant with Neville. The dream. The god. The god who spoke to you. Did he tell you his name?"

"No," she said, looking at me like I was nuts. "It was a dream—not reality."

"I'll be the judge of that," I muttered. "What did he look like?"

"Umm... mossy green hair," she said, wrinkling her brow in thought. "A crown... and I think a scepter."

"Wearing. What was he wearing?" I pressed.

"Well," she said with an embarrassed little laugh. "I believe it was a diaper. I assumed since we were talking about my baby he was sporting a diaper to show solidarity."

Snapping my fingers, I magically placed a pair of sound blocking earmuffs on Neville. I didn't have time to get stabbed right now. And I was about to let it rip.

"Poseidon," I yelled. "The diaper wearing, rum drinking buttdong of a motherfucker was the god in your dreams! This is some kind of set up."

"Pardon me, little swimming hook... Mermaid," Bonar said, catching himself just in time. "But why would Poseidon set ye up? The nut job loves ye like a daughter."

Shit. Bonar was right. The assnard would never set me up to be harmed. However, he was the master of meddling with everyone's fate—especially the ones he loved the most.

"Tell me this," Rick said to Kim as he pulled out his laptop. "The bar you met the Gnomes at to pay the bullshit debt. Is that the bar where you always meet them?"

Kim nodded with wide eyes, not following any of this. The pieces of the puzzle were coming together, but there was a massive hole in the middle.

"The old fart only gave me the name of one bar," Rick said tersely as he searched the notes he'd taken. "I don't think that was a mistake. At all."

"Neither do I," I agreed as I began to pace the kitchen like a Mermaid on a mission. "However, I still have no clue what the connection is. How are Kim and Neville connected to the abductions of the lesser gods?"

I stopped pacing and my stomach roiled.

"What?" Rick demanded, staring at me.

"Do you think the green-haired turd lied? Do you think any lesser gods have been abducted at all?"

Rick's claws popped out and his fangs descended. "I will kick his drunk ass if he's fucking with us," he growled and then turned to me. "But before I make him a soprano, I'll thank him for introducing us."

"Good plan," I acknowledged. "But instead of trying to guess the motives of a butthole who chops his foot off occasionally to mess with the other gods, there's a faster way to get to the bottom of this."

"Holy shit," Rick grunted with a wince. "He chops off his own foot? Why?"

"Too long to explain it. Suffice it to say he does it because Zeus has gastrointestinal issues," I said, dialing the idiot god's number on my cell phone.

"Umm… okaaay," Rick replied, confused.

"It's ringing," I said with excitement.

And then my excitement abated. It went to his voice mail.

Just as I was about to launch my phone out of the window it rang. However, it wasn't the caller I wanted to hear from.

"Dave," I barked into the phone as I rolled my eyes.

"Diane," Dave barked right back, using my fake name which made sense because that was the only name he knew for me. *"First off, thank you for the chocolate flowers. My wife's birthday is today and I forgot to buy her a present. I'm going to re-gift the tasty attractive flowers to her. You're a real life saver. I ate five, but she'll never notice. There has to be at least fifty flowers in the box."*

"Umm…" I said, not sure if I should tell him he'd ingested a butthole. I *had* to. The dolt was about to give assholes to his wife for her birthday. "Dave, those aren't chocolate flowers. They're chocolate buttholes."

There was silence on his end of the call. I didn't blame him. But how was I to know the dumbass was so cheap he was going to re-gift a box of edible buttholes to his wife?

"Not to worry," Dave said. *"Helga won't even notice. She can't see for shit anymore."*

"No pun intended?" I shot back with a gag.

"What's that you say?" he asked.

"Nothing," I replied, shaking my head as Rick laughed

hysterically. Clearly, he was hearing both sides of the conversation. Werewolf auditory skills were insane. "Why are you calling?"

"*Right,*" he said. "*Well, it's a bad fucking day. The insurance company told me to go fuck myself. Bastards won't let me get a plane. They weren't real amused when I told them where they could shove their shitty attitudes... and then they eighty-sixed the show.*"

"They canceled us?" I asked, shocked. Sweet Chicken of the Sea in a whirlpool. How in the heck were we supposed to lure the Gnome King out if we didn't have a damned cooking show anymore? "Won't the network stand behind us?"

"*Nope,*" Dave said. "*Dumb sons of bitches are running scared because we lost the insurance bond. Fuckers won't even take my calls, but that might be because I threatened to crap in their cars and superglue the doors shut.*"

I had nothing to say to that one. I wouldn't take his call either if I were them.

"*It was a good run while it lasted, Diane. I'm gonna try to get my old job back at the Tasty Freeze. Come by and see me sometime. I'll give you and Jack a free ice cream cone.*"

"Umm... will do," I said because I was polite.

"*Oh, and I can't get ahold of Kim. If you see her let her know we're kaput.*"

"I will," I promised. "And Dave?"

"*Yes, Diane?*"

"Thank you."

"*You're most welcome. You and Jack made my blood pressure rise, but it was a damned good time. Take care.*"

"You too," I said as I hung up and flopped down on the couch in defeat. "We're screwed."

"Maybe. Maybe not," Rick said. "We can just drive back up, case the bar and follow the Gnomes by car. Eventually, we'll find the damn Palace."

It was a plan. Not the best plan and not nearly as fun as jumping out of a plane, but at least it was something.

"I just wish we knew where the dang Gnome Palace was," I said, standing up and getting ready to leave.

"Me know," Neville said, pulling the earmuffs off his bulbous head.

Shit. He must have super-duper hearing if he could make out what I had said through the muffs. The little dude was getting one hell of an inappropriate education today.

Kim's head turned sharply towards her son. "How do you know where the Gnome Palace is?"

"Me daddy comes to me in my dreams and he tell me," Neville said with a happy giggle.

"You know your daddy?" Kim whispered with a sad smile.

"Me do!" Neville said. "Last night me daddy say he loves me and he loves you. Me daddy also say Pirate Boooonar is a good man and we can love him. Boooonar will love us forever and ever."

Kim's knees buckled and Bonar caught her in his arms before she hit the floor like a sack of potatoes.

"Neville's pappy came to me in me dreams too," Bonar said, as he carefully laid Kim on the couch and cupped her cheek lovingly. "The salty dog has given me his permission to woo ye. Methinks it would be a fine idea after this is over to take ye and the wee bairn back to the Mystical Isle with me. Are ye all right with that, lovely Kim?"

"I am," Kim whispered through her tears. "I would be honored."

"Aye, then it's done," Bonar said, dancing a spastic little jig of joy.

Shaking my head at the magical irony of all that was transpiring, I sat down next to Neville and snapped my fingers. Pink glitter blew around the room as a detailed map of Tennessee appeared on the kitchen table.

"Can you point to where the Gnome Palace is located?" I asked the little dude as I ruffled his red hair. "It would be really awesome if you could do that for me."

Neville glanced over at his mom and Kim nodded.

"There," he said, placing his chubby finger in the middle of what appeared to be a large forest preserve.

"Are you sure?" Rick asked, snapping a picture of the location with his phone.

"Me sure," Neville said with a huge yawn. "Me tired now. Me take nap."

With that, the little guy toddled over to the stairs and waited for his mom.

"I'll be right back," Kim said, scooping Neville into her arms. "He'll sleep for around two hours. I can help you get ready to leave in a sec."

We didn't need help. We hadn't brought anything with us and whatever we needed I could produce with magic. Rick packed up the rest of breakfast so he could eat it on the drive and I made sure nothing embarrassing or incriminating was left in the man cave.

"Bonar, I have no clue what Rick and I are gonna do, but

that's never stopped either one of us before," I told my friend.

"True," Rick said with a grin, taking my hand in his.

"But if something happens, tell my sisters I love them and tell Poseidon that I will haunt the shit out of his dreams for the rest of his unnatural life," I said.

"Aye, lassie," Bonar said with a bow of respect. "Will do."

"Can I help with anything?" Kim said as she came back down the stairs.

"Nope," I said, hugging her. "We're locked and loaded. You're still a mystery, but we'll get to that soon."

Kim nodded and hugged me tight. "Thank you for everything, Madison. You and Rick have changed our lives for the better. Please be careful."

My grin was huge and Rick's was even wider. Alone we were pretty awesome, but together we fucking rocked.

12

RICK

"Crap, we've been down this road three times," I said in frustration as I pulled up the picture of the map on my phone. Without an address, the GPS wasn't of much help. I knew we were close, I could feel it in my freakin' fangs.

The forest was dense and the wildlife sparse. Gnomes were definitely carnivores. Huge pines and unkempt thorny shrubs swayed ominously in the afternoon summer breeze. It was so dark it was almost impossible to tell if it was day or night. My instinct was to drive Madison right out of the forest and come back alone. However, I was very aware that would not fly with my Mermaid. She was an insane, violent warrior with great knockers. I was a certifiable killing machine when necessary and my Johnson was impressive. Neither of us had a fear gene. Together we were the definition of Hades' worst nightmare.

"Do you think Neville made a mistake?" Madison questioned with concern. "He seemed so sure, but if we can't find it we can always go with plan B."

"Steal a plane and parachute into the Gnome compound?" I asked with a grin.

"Umm... no. I didn't think of that. Although, I like the way your mind works." She paused then gasped. "Sweet Seven Seas in a tsunami, do you think the Gnome Palace has been glamoured so no one can't find it?"

It was an excellent fucking question. We'd arrived in the forest over an hour ago and been driving in circles ever since.

"You. Are. Brilliant," I shouted, stopping the truck and getting out. "You drive."

"Why?" she asked as she scooted over and took the wheel.

"Because I can see through glamours."

Madison's laugh had fast become what I lived for and she busted out a fantastic one. Gods, she made me feel ten feet tall.

"Seriously?"

"Seriously," I confirmed with pride. "However, I have to shift to be able to do it."

"Yessssss," Madison squealed, bouncing up and down in the seat. "I've been dying to see your wolf."

"You have?" I asked, surprised. "I was worried it would freak you out."

She punched me in the arm and rolled her sparkling rose-colored eyes. "You've seen me grow a tail with scales on it and breathe underwater. Why in Poseidon's drunk butt would you think I'd be freaked out by your wolf?"

Gods, this woman was so perfect for me. I was tempted to punch myself in the head to make sure I wasn't dreaming but thought better of it. "Well, he's really big," I told her hesitantly. "My pack never liked him much."

"Your pack sounds like a bunch of jackholes. Is your wolf bigger than your Alpha's wolf?" she inquired with a raised brow.

I nodded.

"There you go, dude. That buttmunch is threatened by you, end of story," Madison snapped, clearly annoyed that I'd been treated badly.

She might have a point. All male Werewolves considered each other brothers, but the Alpha actually was my biological brother. And my brother didn't like me much. The feeling was mutual. Rob was older by a year and was as careful and guarded as I was carefree and adventurous—or *out of fucking control* as my brother liked to put it. I wasn't sure if it was his responsibilities that pissed him off so much or if it was me.

I'd tried and failed repeatedly to be what he wanted me to be. I'd always thought that if I could get back into my pack's good graces that life would be terrific—even perfect. However, that was no longer my dream because a beautiful pink haired girl had seen me for exactly what I was and loved me anyway.

"Is the truck large enough for your wolf?" Madison asked with the excitement of a little kid on Christmas morning.

"Barely, but yes," I told her with a laugh as I pressed the button to open the sunroof. If I could stick my head out, I would fit just fine—tight but fine.

I hadn't shifted in a while and my inner wolf was now clawing at my insides to get out. Maybe I had more in common with my Mermaid than I'd thought. She needed to swim to survive and I needed to run. The bonus was that I'd be even stronger than I was right now if I let my wolf come out for a bit.

"So which plan do we want to go with when we find the Palace?" Madison asked. "I mean, we came up with about ten on the drive, but all of them have big fat hairy holes. Bottom line is that we need to get the lesser gods out and secure Stew the asswipe so Poseidon can de-ball him at a later date. Any incidental destruction is purely an extra."

She was correct. We needed something more solid—something foolproof or at the very least, seriously dangerous. If we were going to bite it while securing a Gnome king to be castrated by a soused, green haired god, I wanted to go down in flames or a massive explosion.

"How about this?" I suggested, pulling a plan out of my ass. I rolled best that way. "I shift and we find the fucker's Palace. We pull up to the gate because all loser Gnome Palaces have gates in fairy tales. I quickly shift back. You magically blow out our tires—and make it loud… *explosive* loud. Poof, we're stranded in front of exactly where we want to be."

"I like it," she said with a nod. "And they'll definitely recognize *Jack and Diane*. Enough of the bastards have been to the show. Someone has to know who we are. We say we were out scouting locations for the new episode—trying to find an area to do a fifty foot-high bonfire to roast s'mores."

"Love it," I shouted and kissed my Mermaid hard. "Then what?"

Madison giggled and shrugged. "No fucking clue. From there we wing it."

"I'm in."

"Show me your wolf, big boy," she purred.

I was sad that we couldn't get in a quickie before we potentially died. However, if we were as close to the Palace as I thought we were, there was a fine chance we could be discovered with our pants down. That was *not* a good plan.

"Wait." Madison put her hand on my arm. "How will we communicate when you shift?"

"One bark go right. Two go left. Three go straight and a growl to stop the vehicle."

"Got it," she said with excitement in her eyes. "Shift. Now."

I did. But first I stripped. I didn't want to shred the shit out of my clothes and have to deal with Gnomes while my Johnson blew in the wind.

Closing my eyes, I let the enchantment take over. I could feel the ancient magic of my ancestors as it flowed through my veins. My bones shifted seamlessly and my skin became dark golden fur. My face elongated, but my eyes stayed the same blue. A feeling of intense freedom washed over me and I chuffed at being stuck in a damn truck. The need to sprint through the forest was overwhelming.

"Gorgeous," Madison whispered in awe as she hesitantly put her hand out to stroke me.

In my shift, I'd almost forgotten she was in the car, but the sound of her voice pulled me right back into reality. All desire to run through the woods disappeared when I saw her sitting next to me with love and admiration in her eyes. My wolf was home with this brave, crazy, and beautiful Mermaid. He knew it and I knew it.

"Can I touch you?" she asked with a smile and a tilt of her head.

Lowering my huge head, I rubbed it against her cheek. My Mermaid sighed with joy and wrapped her arms around my furry neck. She showed no fear. No disappointment. No dislike. It was the first time in a very long time that my wolf was completely at peace.

Well, not completely at peace. It was pissed off that we hadn't bitten our mate yet and made her ours in the way of our kind. That would come soon. Last night wasn't the right time since the mating *bite* caused the mating *frenzy*. We'd need at least a week to get that amount of boinking out of our system.

Right now, we didn't have that kind of time. We had a mission to accomplish and some lesser gods to free. A week of aerobic nookie was on the agenda for later. We just needed to live through the next hour or two.

Sticking my head out of the sunroof, I tensed and growled. Madison turned the car off immediately. There was a very good reason I felt like we were close to the Gnome Palace. We were parked right in front of it. Huge iron gates with the heinous face of the Gnome King carved into them stared menacingly at me.

Shee-ott. I quickly thanked the gods that we'd not been spotted yet. I didn't want to blow my lupine cover unless I had to. Gnomes were violent, but they were also stupid. I wanted them to believe that *Jack and Diane* were human for as long as possible.

Shifting back, I quickly redressed and checked for my explosives and knives. Bingo. I was good to go.

"We're here?" Madison whispered.

"We are definitely fucking here."

"All I see are trees and bushes," she said, peering out of the window.

"That's all I can see now too," I told her, feeling my adrenaline spike. "However, once they see us and take us through the gates we should be able to see everything."

"How do you know all of this?" she asked as she prepared to blow out the tires.

"Unfortunately, I've fought the Gnomes before. They have hidden compounds like this all over the world. It's why most humans think the Gnomes are a myth."

"Got it," Madison said, checking her weapons. "Kill spots?"

"Removal of the head, of course," I told her. "But you can also go for the nards. A solid kick or a heavy blast of magic to the nuts will render them helpless for about thirty minutes. A dagger will work too."

"Duuuude," Madison said with a roll of her eyes. "That's the same for all males who get racked."

"Trust me on this," I told her with a laugh. "They curl up into a ball like a roly-poly bug and scream like a fucking girl the entire time they're down. However, their nards are tiny and you have to get a direct hit."

"You're shitting me," Madison said with a laugh.

"I shit you not," I shot right back grinning. "It's the gods' honest truth."

"You ready?" she asked with a wild look of excitement in her eyes.

"Born ready," I replied.

And then the plans changed. Drastically.

ROBYN PETERMAN

"Mooomaid? Waaawuf?" came a little voice from the very back of the SUV.

"*What the fuck?*" I hissed as I whipped my head to the left and spotted a happily waving Neville.

"Ohhhh shitshitshitshitshit," Madison said in a panic. "I'm seriously cool with risking my own life, but not Neville's."

"Ditto," I said, reaching for the alien dude and pulling his little body onto my lap. "Start the truck. We have the get the hell out of here."

"On it," Madison said and then froze. "Incoming."

She paled considerably and pointed to six Gnomes headed our way.

"Gods damn it," I snarled and tried to shove the child under the front seat.

"We can't leave him in the car," Madison said, freaking out.

I wanted to join her freak out, but we had to think quick. "We can't walk in with him. They want him dead."

"Oh yes we can," she said as she waved her hands and a large backpack appeared.

Grabbing Neville and kissing him on the head she went nose to nose with him. "Right now we're not going to discuss that it was a really poopy thing to do to stow away in the truck. Your mommy is gonna have a dang fit. You're going to get into the backpack and Rick is going to carry you on his back."

"I am?" I asked.

"You are," Madison confirmed as she gently but quickly helped the little alien dude into the pack. "Neville, you can't

130

make a sound. This is very important and you have to obey me. Please."

"Me will, Mooomaid," Neville said with huge terrified eyes, not quite as proud of his choice to come along now.

"Text Bonar on my phone," Madison instructed me as she helped me put the backpack on. "We have an app called Find My Friends. Bonar will be able to find us as long as I have my phone on me."

"That's brilliant," I said as I quickly texted Bonar and alerted him to the shit show about to happen.

The Gnomes were almost on us and they didn't look pleased. While normally that would thrill me to the nth degree. Right now it sucked every kind of ass and then some.

"You ready, *Diane*?" I asked through clenched teeth as I smiled and waved at the fast approaching fuckers.

"Do I have a choice, *Jack*?" Madison shot back just as tersely.

"Nope."

"Then I'm ready. Let's do this shit."

13

MADISON

STORMING THE TRUCK WITH SPEED THAT SHOOK THE FLOOR OF the forest, the Gnomes looked ready for the kill. They surrounded the SUV with their weapons drawn. It was a very fucking bad situation considering our stowaway. Under other circumstances, I would have gone to town on their disgusting asses, but that wasn't going to happen today. Our hands were tied with a baby on board.

The guards were in Gnome form standing about seven feet tall with enormous fangs and oversized heads. Their bodies were covered in wiry hair and their backs were hunched. For centuries, they'd screwed with humans pretending to be the elusive Bigfoot. All of the members of the Sasquatch population that I knew were seriously put out by this since they were far more attractive than the Gnomes —*attractive* being a relative word.

And the smell… it was some serious stank.

Growling, hissing and gnashing their fangs they aimed their firepower at the truck.

"Can you see their nards?" Rick whispered while still smiling and waving at the irate Gnomes.

Peering at the abominations, I squinted my eyes. They didn't wear any clothes when in their Gnome form but honestly, they had so much fur they didn't really need apparel. The only hairless part of a Gnome's body was the face and hair might have been an improvement.

"Umm... no. Can you?" I asked, squinting harder.

"Sadly, yes," he said with a gag. "Look for the small hairy pickle."

Again, I looked. "Like a Kosher dill or a midget sweet pickle?" I questioned still searching.

"Midget sweet pickle," Rick confirmed. "If you can find that, the miniscule nards are on either side. I did warn you they were itsy bitsy."

"No wonder they're so pissed," I said with a muffled laugh as I finally found something that resembled a fuzzy mini midget sweet pickle flanked by two eensy-weensy hairy peas. "These dudes really got screwed over in the junk department."

"Ya think?" Rick said with a chuckle.

"Get out of the vehicle and put your hands in the air," the Gnome in the front snarled, banging violently on the window with the butt of his enormous rifle.

"Damn good thing bullets won't kill us," Rick muttered as he went to open the door.

"True," I said, reaching for my handle and then stopped. "But we have no clue if guns can kill Neville. If he really is half human, he could die easily."

"Fuck," Rick muttered and closed his eyes for a second. "Madison, we have to play it safe."

My heart beat a rapid tattoo in my chest and my stomach clenched in terror. Safe wasn't a word in my vocabulary. "Can we do that?" I asked, alarmed. I didn't even know what that meant.

"No choice," he said, swiping the sweat from his forehead and shuddering. "Never done it, but there's a first time for everything, baby. Main objective… get Neville out of here alive. If we can free the lesser gods and incarcerate Stew for his eventual de-peckering, great. If not, we'll have to come back."

I nodded in agreement. "You got any more to the plan? Like how we're gonna do it?"

Rick glanced over and grinned. It was wildly inappropriate to get turned on at a time like this but I did. I had it *bad* for the Werewolf.

"We're gonna wing it."

"Roger that, captain. Let's play it *safe*."

"May the gods be with us so we don't blow anything up."

And then all hell broke loose.

However, it wasn't at all the hell we'd expected. At all.

"*Jack and Diane?*" the biggest and ugliest Gnome squeaked as he began to hop up and down causing several trees to uproot and crash to the ground.

"Oh my GODS!" another one shouted and then passed out in rabid excitement.

Two others began to tremble and weep as they went for their cell phones and begged for selfies with us. It was freakin' surreal. Poseidon had been correct about Gnomes loving their cooking shows. Luckily, we were no longer in the SUV because it was now just a crushed heap of metal under a massive cedar tree. I sent a silent thank you to Zeus that we hadn't left Neville under the seat.

For the next thirty minutes, we posed for pictures with five shrieking Gnomes. The one who'd passed out was going to be devastated if the hero worship of the others was anything to judge by. We were freakin' rock stars. The one thing I was grateful for was that the bastard who'd tried to hit Kim wasn't amongst them. And thankfully, Neville didn't make a sound.

"Sooooo, Jack and Diane?" Bart, the largest Gnome, gushed. "What brings you to our neck of the woods?"

"Well, Bart," Rick said, slapping him on the back and sending him flying. "We're scouting locations for our next episode."

Bart was thrilled to have been decked by *Jack*. He hopped right back up and knelt at Rick's and my feet.

"We would be honored, thrilled, delighted, and humbled if you'd like to use the compound as your next location," Bart blabbered.

"Where exactly are we?" I inquired with my megawatt TV smile turned up to the max.

"You don't know?" one called Tiny asked.

"Umm… nope. We just looooove the area—very dark and umm… interestingly scented," I said, glancing over at the backpack on Rick's back to make sure it wasn't moving. "And now that the network has canceled our show, we have to do everything ourselves."

"WHAT?" Bart screamed and began to throw a temper tantrum that would make a two year old proud. "They can't cancel the show. We LOVE the show. We have it running repeatedly in the rec room of the Gnome recreation center. I've seen all ten episodes three hundred times apiece."

"Holy fuck," Rick muttered under his breath. "Gonna be like taking candy from a baby."

"Don't jinx us," I whispered as I patted Bart on his hairy back while he kicked and screamed on the ground. "Maybe you guys can help us since you're such *big* and hairy fans."

"Tell us what you want and need," Tiny begged picking up Bart and dropkicking him into the woods so he could be closer to me. "Your wish is our command, O Great Diane."

The stench was almost debilitating, but the offer was pure gold.

"How about a tour of the Palace so we can find the best place to shoot?" I suggested.

"Done," Bart yelled as he jogged back over and pummeled Tiny in retaliation for booting him like a rag doll. "Follow me."

"And me," Tiny grunted as he dragged the still unconscious Gnome fan behind him.

We followed them through a gate we couldn't see and then the hell of the Gnome compound came into crystal clear and very heinous focus. As far as the eye could see, everything was rundown and in horrid disrepair—well, everything except the Palace. It was pristine.

"What the hell?" Rick mumbled as he too took in the horrible living conditions the King made his subjects live in.

It made the side of town Kim had been living in look like paradise.

"This is so sad," I whispered, again checking on Neville.

He was as quiet as a mouse and hadn't moved a muscle. Kim must be shitting her pants. I knew I would be.

"May we carry your load?" Bart offered politely reaching for the backpack.

"NO," Rick shouted as Bart shrank back like a beaten puppy. Rick tilted his head to the side in confusion at Bart's meek reaction. "I mean, thank you, Bart but no. I'm just fine. I'm carrying precious cargo and it can't leave my body."

Bart nodded and grinned with relief, clearly happy that Rick wasn't mad at him. "Apple pies flambé?"

I laughed and shook my head. "Possibly," I told him as a plan began to hatch in my head. Even if we could just accomplish part of the mission while keeping Neville safe, that would be better than nothing. "We're looking for someplace a little dark and scary for the next episode. You know, a seriously creepy area. Maybe a room with chains and cages... instruments of torture would be all kinds of awesome. I'm planning to juggle watermelons over an enormous vat of bubbling water filled with sharks while Rick throws daggers and slices the watermelon while it's in the air."

"Who's Rick?" Tiny asked, confused.

Shitshitshit.

"Rick's my *middle* name. On TV I go by Jack. *Diane* here likes to call me Rick and my friends calls me *Jack Rick with the enormous dick*," Rick said, giving me a raised yet victorious eyebrow.

I was speechless. It took everything I had not to laugh. Rick had just bailed my ass out of what could have been a deadly mess, but the enormous dick part was almost too much. True, but too much.

"We would be honored to call you Jack Rick with the

enormous dick," Bart said, bowing low to my insane Werewolf.

"Fine by me, boys," Rick said with a mischievous grin pulling at his mouth. "And Diane's middle name is Madison. On TV she goes by Diane. I like to call her Madison. However," he stated, enjoying himself far too much. "Her friends like to call her Madison Diane with the bootylicious can."

If I wasn't playing it *safe*, I would have stabbed the wolf in the ass—five times. However, I had to be content with just rolling my eyes.

"Thank you, Rick the dick," I said sweetly with a smile. That moniker would stick.

"My pleasure," he replied, grinning wide. "And that's Jack Rick with the enormous dick."

"Riiiight. My bad, Enormous Dick."

I supposed this was as dangerous as we were going to get. At least it was funny.

"May we call you Madison Diane with the bootylicious can?" Tiny asked shyly.

I swallowed hard so I didn't punch the Gnome in the head or laugh. "Of course," I choked out. "We're friends, aren't we?"

"Absolutely," he said, skipping in a circle.

Others joined him, and in a matter of minutes we were surrounded by at least fifty skipping Gnomes. What in the Chicken of the Sea was happening here? Gnomes weren't supposed to skip and be sweet. They were evil bastards who belonged in Hades and sent body parts of lesser gods to Poseidon.

"I'm a little confused," Rick said, through barely moving lips as he waved to the ecstatic crowd.

"I'm a lot confused," I replied, doing my best pageant wave. "These people are pathetic. They're not killers."

"Agreed," he said, scratching his head.

"Not all Gnomes bad," a little voice whispered. "Only ones with King. Most Gnomes poor and sad. Me daddy tell me so."

My head snapped to the backpack and then back to the prancing Gnomes. Thank the gods, no one seemed to hear Neville.

"Shhhh," I hissed, keeping my smile plastered on my face. "Did you hear that?" I asked Rick. He nodded and made a sour face.

"What?" I looked around for trouble, but saw none. "Are you okay?"

"Yes. I'm fine. However, Neville either peed or drooled."

Biting back my grin, I felt only a little bit bad that Jack Rick with the enormous dick was the one wearing the backpack. The Gnomes had started to sing for us. I had a feeling my ears might bleed, but thought it would be rude to slap my ears over them. My mom taught me it was far easier to be nice than mean. Plus, I could regenerate my eardrums in a hot second.

The singing—or heinous noise to be more accurate— made it easier for Rick and me to communicate.

"Going out on a limb here," Rick said softly. "But I think most of the Gnomes here are victims—not evil."

"Agreed," I said, wincing at a particularly high note Bart let rip. "When you battled the Gnomes, did they behave like this?"

"Nope. They didn't look like these freaks either—much bigger. Much uglier. Much meaner."

"Mmmkay," I said, scanning the bombed out looking village that surrounded the Palace. "How about we stick with the nice ones, get to the lesser gods and then let Poseidon deal with Stew the Gnome bastard King?" I suggested.

"On any other day I would disagree," Rick whispered. "However, since my back has been used as a potty and I'd like to take a shower, I'm gonna go with your *safe* plan."

I giggled and he grinned. He was going to be a great daddy someday.

"So I take it you think the lesser gods are in a dungeon?" he asked.

"Well, since everything here is like a bad flippin' fairy tale, I'm going with a yes," I told him.

"If I have to listen to any more Gnome tunes, I might pee my pants like our little alien buddy did. You ready to tour the bowels of the Palace?"

"Born ready, Rick the dick," I said, giving him a thumbs up.

"Umm… you left part of my name out," he reminded me.

"Nope. I didn't."

Flouncing ahead of my Werewolf before he could argue the point further, I took Bart's hand and headed toward the Palace. Bart was so excited by my gesture, he cried. The Gnome cried big huge tears that smelled a little like three-day-old garbage left in the sun but I simply held my breath and smiled.

I was a Mermaid. I could hold my breath for a week. I giggled as I watched Rick try not to heave as Tiny put a hairy arm around his shoulder and marched him up the path.

While we might be playing it *safe*, it was anything but safe for our olfactory senses...

14

RICK

"Is something wrong, gentlemen?" I asked our large hairy tour guides as they exchanged hushed words and worried glances.

"No," Bart said with a forced laugh that I was sure was laced with terror. "Nothing at all, Jack Rick with the enormous dick. Nothing at all, my friend."

As soon as we'd hit the manicured main path that led to the Palace, all fifty Gnomes who had been happily trailing us, scattered and disappeared—all but Bart and Tiny. Madison's eyes had narrowed for a moment as we watched the crowd hustle away in abject fear.

"Something is very fishy in Gnome land," she whispered as we followed an uncomfortable Bart and a shaky Tiny.

"Agreed." I adjusted the backpack full of Neville on my very wet back. "Do not take a crap," I hissed quietly over my shoulder. "If you have to poop, you'd better hold it. You feel me?"

The little alien dude moved around just a little and giggled softly.

I took that as a yes. It was one thing to be peed on. It was another thing entirely to walk around smelling like shit when it wasn't your fault. However, the Gnomes smelled liked baked ass so a Neville dump probably wouldn't even be noticed.

Where the town was in squalor, the grounds of the Palace were anything but. In the distance, I spotted a crew of emaciated Gnomes tending to the immaculate flowerbeds and the shrubs. The Gnomes seemed broken and hopeless. The more I saw—the angrier I got.

"Excuse me, Tiny? Bart?" Madison said as politely as ever. "Why are we going around to the back of the Palace and not through the front door?"

Both Gnomes froze and then pulled us under a weeping Mulberry tree to hide from prying eyes. Tiny was wringing his huge hands and Bart was systematically yanking strands of wiry hair out of his right elbow. It looked seriously painful.

"Are you not supposed to be in the Palace?" Madison asked, gently stopping Bart from picking his elbow bald.

"Not exactly," Tiny hedged, making no eye contact whatsoever. "We just like to use a different entrance. Much easier access to the area that would be appropriate for your show."

"I see," I said, not wanting to beat around the bush. I had no clue how soon Neville would need to take a leak again. This show needed to get on the road. "So if we went up to the front door and knocked, that would be a problem?"

Bart went positively ashen and Tiny almost fainted. That pretty much answered the question.

"You wouldn't want to do that Jack Rick with the enormous dick," Bart choked out. "Nononononono, not smart."

"Because?" Madison pressed.

"Well, we're very forward thinking even though we've never been off the compound," Tiny explained.

"Whoa dude," I said, squinting at him. "You've never been off this property? How old are you?"

"Two hundred," Tiny told us. "Bart is a hundred and seven. And no one has ever been off the compound. It's forbidden."

Attacking his left elbow now, Bart joined the bizarre and unbelievable conversation. "That's not exactly true. There are those who are allowed off the compound, but not us."

"The Gnomes we've met so far," Madison said, again pulling Bart's hand off his elbow. "Have any of them left the compound?"

"Ohhhhhh no." Tiny shook his head so hard I thought his brains might fall out of his ears. "We're the Undesirables. We are prohibited from contact with the rest of the world. We are unworthy. Lower than low. Scum of the earth."

"Says who?" I ground out through clenched teeth.

"The King," Bart said reverently, bowing his head.

Madison was pissed and her fingers began to spark. Quickly shoving them into her pockets, she pressed for more. "So who *is* allowed off the compound?"

Tiny peeked through the leaves that surrounded us to make sure he wouldn't be heard. "The King's army. One hundred of the bravest and most important Gnomes in existence. They are free to come and go as they please."

I could barely stop myself from growling. This was *fucked up*. So the only Gnomes I'd ever come into contact with were in the King's *army*. Clearly, they were the same fuckers that had been forcing Kim to pay for the little pee alien's existence.

"Jack Rick with the enormous dick and Madison Diane with the bootylicious can, we must hurry before we're noticed," Bart said, also peeking through the leaves.

"Why are you doing this for us?" I asked. "If you could be punished for being in the castle, why are you risking it?"

Bart and Tiny smiled. The first real smile I'd seen. It was alarmingly unattractive but pretty damned nice at the same time.

"You are our heroes," Bart said as his beady eyes filled with smelly and heartfelt tears. "You and Madison Diane with the bootylicious can have saved us. Watching your bravery and the way you almost decapitate each other while cooking delicious food has made our lives worth living."

"Cooking shows are the only TV we are permitted," Tiny added. "I'm very fond of Martha Stewart and Snoop Dog, but *Bitchin' in the Kitchen'* changed my life for the better. The way you blew up half the studio and then did the breakdancing number on the hot coals while roasting marshmallows impaled on your fingers still gives me chills. I just can't believe…"

"Can't believe what?" I asked, preening a bit about his love of the breakdancing episode. It was my idea. However, Madison came up with the hot coals and marshmallow part. She was fucking brilliant. Together we were unstoppable.

Tiny lowered his voice so much we had to lean in.

"I can't believe that you're *human*."

Bart quickly checked the area for eavesdroppers. We were definitely *not* human—not even close. But I didn't think it was prudent to reveal that yet. Gnomes were not the sharpest tools in the shed.

"Humans are bad?" Madison asked as she too scanned the area through the leaves.

"Not in my book," Bart said.

"Mine either," Tiny said, getting more nervous by the second. "But if the Palace finds out you're here it won't be good."

"The King hates humans?" I asked, already knowing the answer. He'd killed his own son because he'd consorted with a human.

Both men nodded in embarrassment.

"Why?" I asked, hoping to learn something useful here to take the King down. "What have humans ever done to him?"

For the umpteenth time, the two exchanged terrified glances.

"The heir to the throne—the good and noble Gnome Dirk —was lured away by a human woman and begat a child with her," Tiny explained.

"And because of this horrible crime against nature, his father, and our kind, Dirk was put to death," Bart finished sadly, swiping a rank tear from his eye. "Dirk was a wonderful Gnome. Since his death, it has gotten more difficult for the Undesirables here. Noble Gnome Dirk didn't believe in divided societies. He believed everyone was equal —even humans."

"And King Stew doesn't believe that," I said flatly.

Bart's voice was a mere whisper. "No. He does not."

My backpack moved. I was very aware that Neville was hearing all of this. I hated that for him, but life was tough sometimes. I was glad that they spoke highly of Dirk.

"Do you think it's bad to consort with humans?" Madison questioned. "What if Dirk had fallen in love with this human woman?"

"Then I say good for him," Tiny whispered with a little grin that wasn't too revolting. "And I hope that someday the child comes back and knocks the King off the throne and leads us to salvation."

"Tiny," Bart hissed as he punched his cohort in the head. "Don't speak like that. What you said is punishable by death. You know this. Dirk is gone forever and no one will save us. We are not worthy of saving."

My backpack was now wriggling like it was full of Mexican jumping beans. Turning so the Gnomes couldn't see it, I reached back and put my hand on Neville. The child actually *had* come back. But I sure as hell wasn't going to let my little alien buddy have a go at the man who had killed the boy's father. The Gnome King would eat someone like Neville for breakfast.

And of course, the only thanks I got for my noble thought was another hot stream of pee down my back. My Mermaid knew what she was doing when she made me carry the backpack...

"Take us to the dungeon and we'll talk some more," Madison said.

Tiny nodded his head and Bart spoke. "As you wish Madison Diane with the bootylicious can."

15

MADISON

THE DUNGEON WAS RIGHT OUT OF MY WORST NIGHTMARES—dark, dank, and filled with instruments of torture. The air was cold and ominous and the place reeked of sadness and pain. It was awful, it was terrifying ... *and it was empty*.

Shit.

Exchanging a cryptic look with Rick, I said a quick prayer to the gods that the prisoners hadn't already been put to death. If we were too late after all this, I was going to lose my seashells on everyone—and no one wanted to see that.

We'd entered through what I could only call a rusted out manhole on the back side of the Palace and then made our way in through several rodent infested tunnels. I walked behind Rick to protect Neville from any unwanted visitors who might try to hitch a ride in the backpack.

It took about a half hour. The boys apologized profusely and repeatedly. I told them it was fine. This was what I had asked to see. It wasn't their fault.

"Are you certain you want to film down here?" Bart

asked with a shiver of discomfort. "You're much too famous and classy to hang out where the King keeps his prisoners."

"Does he have any prisoners at the moment?" I asked casually as I examined the spikes and mallets used for the gods only knew what.

"We wouldn't know," Tiny said, looking away from the rack and the thumbscrews with a shudder. "The Undesirables are not privy to the goings on of our King and his army."

I couldn't believe what I was seeing... or hearing. The Gnome King was one sick motherhumper. The iron maiden with the inward facing spikes made me feel ill. The stake for burning people alive was positively horrid. And the iron plates were most likely used for some kind of torture that I didn't even want to imagine.

Was this the shit was he'd been using on the lesser gods? Ripping Stew's pecker off and feeding it to him didn't sound like such a bad plan after all.

"Is this the only dungeon?" Rick asked, shaking his head in disgust at what he was seeing.

"Yes," Bart said. "But this is only one side of it. The other side is locked with magic."

Bingo. I'd bet my tail that the other side housed the people we were looking for. Glancing over at the Gnomes, I sighed. In the insanely short time I'd known them, Bart and Tiny had grown on me like a weird, bad smelling, but quite lovely fungus. I wanted them out of here. This was not their problem. They had enough problems without getting killed or tortured for aiding us.

"Bart and Tiny," I said, staring up at both of the huge

Gnomes wearing my *I'm the boss* expression. "You are going to go back to the village now. You feel me?"

"Ohhhh no!" Tiny cried out. "We will never leave your side while you're here. It's far too dangerous for humans like you. And we love you."

"We're not human," Rick said flatly. "And umm... thank you for loving us, but I can't really say the feeling is mutual. Although, I like you—a lot. You're much different than the other fuckers of your kind that I've come across in the past. The whole Undesirable thing is bullshit. You are far more desirable than your assnardfucker of a King. And yes... I'm aware that your nuts are the size of blueberries, but you need to man up and take that bastard down."

They stared at Rick with blank gazes. He'd confused the shit out of the poor Gnomes.

"Jack Rick with the enormous dick, it makes my heart sing that you like us a lot, but you have no clue what you are dealing with in our land. Going against King Stew and his army will ensure a very long and painful death. There is much evil here and you *are* human," Bart said, perplexed.

"Not human," I said, echoing Rick.

"Are," Tiny insisted, shrugging helplessly. "Please... this day is the most wonderful in my entire life. I will not walk away and let the two that have brought me thousands of hours of pleasure die."

"Sweet Poseidon in a mankini," Madison said with a giggle. "How many times did you watch the ten episodes?"

"A lot," Tiny admitted sheepishly.

"We're staying," Bart insisted.

"You're leaving," Rick corrected him.

Both of the Gnomes stood their ground and narrowed their eyes.

"This is going to be a lesson in tough love, Jack Rick with the enormous dick and Madison Diane with the bootylicious can," Tiny barked, crossing his massive hairy arms over his bulbous chest. "It is very obvious that you two wonderful people are not right in the head. No one in their sane mind would ever blowtorch popcorn on the chest of your cohost while drinking a piña colada blindfolded."

"That was a good time," I remembered aloud as Rick gave me a thumbs up and a wink.

"I did love that episode," Bart gushed like the rabid fan he was. "However, Tiny is right. In your batshit crazy minds, you have somehow convinced yourselves that you're not human."

"Well," Rick said with a chuckle. "You got that right."

"Finally," Tiny huffed out with relief.

"Not the human part," I said with a laugh. "You nailed the batshit crazy part."

And that's when both the huge and smelly Gnomes began to cry.

"Shit," Rick said, closing his eyes and running his hands through his hair. "We're gonna have to prove it. Can you be trusted, boys?"

Swiping at their eyes and nodding their heads they crossed their hearts and promised.

"I'm the president of your fan club," Tiny offered. "We're the Di-acks! Get it? Combo of both your names."

"We have a fan club?" I asked, shocked and kind of flattered.

Nodding spastically, Bart grinned. "You do and I'm the

vice-president slash secretary. We would be happy to become blood brothers with you if that would prove our loyalty."

Both Gnomes bit down on their hands with their sharp fangs and held their bloody appendages out to us. Thick green goo dripped off the wounds and I puked a little in my mouth.

"Ahhh… no. I'm good. Madison?" Rick inquired with a gag, grossed out at the thought of exchanging blood with the Gnomes who ran our *fan club*.

"Good here too," I choked out.

Rick shrugged and gave me a lopsided grin. "Time to show the *Di-acks* we mean what we say."

"So be it," I said, raising my hands high and slashing them through the air.

In a blast of sparkling pink glitter, all of the instruments of torture morphed into a colorful playground for toddlers. I knew Neville would probably love it, but that was something we could *not* find out right now. I trusted Tiny and Bart, but not enough to let them in on the Neville secret.

The iron maiden was gone and in its place was a bright blue and orange swing set. The stake had become a ball pit filled with hundreds of hot pink squishy balls. There was now a slide, a sandbox and even monkey bars. Gone was every single piece of torture equipment that had lived there for centuries. And of course, there was a kiddie pool. No Mermaid worth her salt would create a play area without a swimming pool.

Tiny and Bart were shocked to complete silence. But we weren't done.

Rick let his fangs drop and his claws pop out. Carefully

handing me the backpack, he shed his clothes and let his wolf take over. Gone was my sexy man and in his place on four legs stood my massive beautiful wolf.

Tiny and Bart were still mute.

"So, friends," I said, smiling up at them. "Will you go back to the village now so you'll be safe?"

"You're not human," Bart said in a daze, eyeing the playground like a child who had never seen one.

"Not human," I confirmed. "Rick is obviously a Werewolf and I'm a Mermaid."

"Ohhhhh," Tiny said, finding his voice and hopping up and down in excitement. "How thrilling. Wait," he said, scratching his head. "Are you really here to scout a location?"

Rick nodded his head for me to answer the question as he morphed back to his human form, dressed and gently put the backpack back on.

"No. But the show did get canceled," I said. "Your assnardfucker of a King kidnapped some lesser gods and the *not so lesser gods* are seriously pissed. Soooo, if you don't want the wrath of Poseidon, Zeus, Apollo, Hades and the rest of the nutty bastards to rain down on you, you should just walk away now and let us do what we came to do."

"You've come to save the lesser gods?" Bart asked.

"We have," Rick said. "Go home. We'll get them out and leave. No one will ever know you were involved. Cool?"

"Not cool," Tiny grunted indignantly and puffed out his furry chest. "I despise our assnardfucker King. And I'm not afraid to say it anymore. Death would be better than living like we do. If you can go on live TV and dare each other to eat ghost peppers while running on a treadmill and reciting the lyrics to ACDC's *Back in Black* backwards, I can be true to myself too. King Stew killed my family and he killed the noble heir to the throne, Dirk. Dirk was the only hope of us ever getting to leave the compound and live a normal life. I will help you and I don't care if I die. If I perish serving the two who have made my life less agonizing with their death-defying cooking, I will die an honorable death."

"Can I add something?" Bart inquired.

"Sure," I said, a bit dazed from Tiny's diatribe.

"While we're all being upfront and open with each other, I'd like to start out by telling you I enjoy wearing women's underpants," Bart announced as Tiny patted his friend on the back nodded for him to continue. "This of course, is punishable by death because our assnardfucker King says so. The gods made me this way and I'm coming out of the closet today."

"Umm... Bart?" Tiny asked, seemingly confused.

"Yes?"

"You're gay?"

"No, not that I have an issue with that," Bart assured all of us. "I like the ladies. I simply enjoy wearing their knickers —very silky and comfortable."

"Anything else?" Rick asked, wincing.

"No," Bart said, shaking his big head. "No. I'm good now."

"Alrighty then," I said, thinking that the Gnomes had Pirates beat in the weird department— hands down. "How about you show us the locked area and then you stand guard while we do the dirty work?"

"It would be a great honor to protect you," Bart said with a bow.

"And it would be a great honor to be protected by you," I replied as I hugged both of the stinky giants.

And I meant it. I now needed a shower as much as Jack did, but I didn't care. Pee and BO were not permanent... friendships were.

16

RICK

IT TOOK MADISON'S MAGIC, MY CLAWS AND FANGS FOLLOWED BY a giant stinky push from the Gnomes to break the iron door down, but we did it. Bart and Tiny stood guard at the entrance and my Mermaid and I went in to see if we'd hit the jackpot.

"Rick," Madison said, stopping me with a touch before we got to the caged area.

"Yes, baby?"

She smiled and cupped my cheek. "I love you. I think you're the smartest, craziest, sexiest and most wonderful man I've ever met. But..."

Wait. There was a *but*? Was I being dumped? My stomach roiled and I wanted to die. This was worse than being banished most of my life. My pack didn't matter to me. Madison did. Without even trying, the Mermaid had become my reason to live.

"But?" I repeated and held my breath as I waited for the blow that would kill me dead.

"But I don't want to get married," she said quickly. "I'd prefer to live in sin with you for the rest of eternity. My sister's wedding was a fucking shit show and I just can't do it... Are you okay with that?"

The breath I exhaled was the most fabulous breath that had ever left my lungs. My body felt as light as a feather and I wanted to sing even though I was tone deaf.

"Yesssss," I said, sagging in relief.

Madison gave me a strange look and nudged me with her elbow. "What did you think I was going to say?"

"I thought you were breaking up with me," I admitted.

"Never," she said, wrapping her arms around me and hugging me tight. "Never ever ever."

"I'm holding you to that, Mermaid," I said, reaching around and unzipping the backpack so Neville could get some fresh air. "You okay little alien dude?"

"Me good," Neville whispered, popping his oversized head out. "Me love Bart and Tiny."

"Me do too," Madison said with a smile as she kissed Neville's chubby cheek. "You are being such a good boy. I'm proud of you."

"Someday me come here and save Bart and Tiny," Neville promised.

Both Madison and I were silent. There was nothing we could say. If that was indeed Neville's destiny, he would have to follow it. I just hoped that he wasn't half human. The little dude would never defeat the Gnome King if he was.

"Neville," Madison said in an odd tone. "Tilt your head to the right, please."

I could feel Madison examining the child. Neville giggled as she ran her hands through his hair.

"Did you find something besides toddler urine?" I asked.

"His hair," she said, removing the backpack from my back. "Look at this and tell me if I'm nuts."

"We both know you're nuts," I said with a chuckle. "It's one of the reasons I love you."

Squatting down I peered at the top of Neville's head and was stunned. It was such a distinctly recognizable color there was no missing it.

"No fucking way," I whispered as I touched the silky strands.

"That's what I thought," Madison said with her adorable nose wrinkled in thought. "How can this be explained?"

"Don't know. Maybe we should ask," I said, sitting down on the floor and getting down to Neville's level. "Little dude, are you part human?"

"No, silly Waaawuf. Me not human at all," he said with a very impressive eye roll for someone his age.

"Are you a merman?" Madison asked, still fixated on his hair.

Neville giggled. "Me a god *and* a Gnome."

And now the hair made sense. And the cryptic reasons behind the mission began to make sense. The bar we'd been sent to made sense and the fact that Kim was our stage manager made sense. The soused bastard had meddled in everyone's life. But I still wasn't sure why.

"How do you know you're a god?" Madison asked, sounding shell shocked.

"Me dreams. Me great-great-great-great-great-great-great-great-great-great-great-great-great-great-great-great-great-great-great-Grand Pappy tell me so."

"And what is your great times umm… whatever Grand

Pappy's name?" I asked, knowing what he was about to share.

Neville leaned in and touched my nose with a chubby finger. "Pooooseidon."

The mossy green strands of hair on his head mixed with the red were hereditary. The fact that the little guy could swim and talk underwater was also hereditary. The eventuality that the little alien dude would be a force to reckoned with in the future was a given. Neville had the bloodline of a king and a god. Holy shit, he might actually come back and save Bart and Tiny.

"Why? How?" Madison said, stroking Neville's head.

"Poseidon's a randy bastard and gods mate with humans all the time," I said, still trying to piece it all together.

"So Kim's parents had to have been Mer-people. And part of their destiny was to move to Tennessee so that Kim would fulfill her destiny," Madison said sadly. "And they withered away because they were landlocked."

Her beautiful rose colored eyes filled with tears and she let her chin fall to her chest. Wrapping both her and the pee stained Neville in my arms, I held them close.

"I don't understand how Kim can survive being landlocked," I said, burying my face in Madison's pink locks.

"If a destiny has been ordained by the gods, the body will acclimate," Madison said. "My guess is that Kim will discover her true nature when she moves to the Mystical Isle."

"Will my zoo be cool on the Mystical Isle?" I asked, feeling a little pushy and uncertain. However, I wasn't going to live in the backwoods of Kentucky if the love of my immortal life was on a fucking island.

Madison glanced up at me with surprised delight in her eyes. "I was going to offer to move into the woods with you."

"Nope," I told my beautiful nut bag. "I'd like to live on the beach for a few centuries. I can shift and run anywhere."

"The zoo will fit in fine," she promised with a giggle. "It's a zoo there already—just without fur."

"Perfect. Do you think there are any lesser gods in this dungeon?" I asked as I pulled her to her feet and we tucked Neville safely back into the pack.

"There's only one way to find out," Madison replied, grimacing.

"Let's do it."

And we did.

17

MADISON

SIX LESSER GODS SAT CHAINED IN FILTHY CAGES AND THEY
didn't look good. The chains clearly prohibited magic or the
cages never would have held them. They sported missing
appendages and were bruised and bloody.

Poseidon hadn't lied, but as usual he omitted a bunch of
details. This side of the dungeon was far more updated than
the other side, but no less inhumane. The gods were missing
body parts, but they would grow back. However, there was
one prisoner here who was not a god at all.

"Petunia?" I blurted out in shock as I stared at my cousin
who I hadn't seen in at least a century. She was a wild child
and a half. Actually, if there ever was a swimming hooker, it
was Petunia. "What in the ever-lovin' Seven Seas are you
doing in the dungeon of the Gnome Palace?"

"Funny you should ask," Petunia said with an enormous
eye roll. "But first off, you look ahhhhhmazing, Madison!"

"Thank you," I squealed. Petunia was a gorgeous

redhead and a compliment from my cousin was rare. "I'm in love."

"With the hot guy wearing a backpack who smells like wee-wee?" she asked with a raised brow.

"Umm... yes," I said, wanting to smack her.

I also wanted to explain why my man smelled funky, but Neville was still a secret. Until I had a knee to nuts conversation with Poseidon, anything related to the little dude was off limits—even to my cousin.

"Okay," Rick said, giving Petunia the stink eye for insulting him. "We're getting all of you out of here. If we unchain you, can you transport yourselves back to Mount Olympus?"

A chorus of disgruntled, snippy, and pissed off *yesses* came back and I rolled my eyes. Did they think we were going to bust their uppity asses out and they fly them home on a magic carpet that we yanked out of our butts? After the shit we'd been through, ungrateful lesser gods were not working for me.

"You know what Rick?" I said, rolling my neck and flipping off the rude lesser gods. "I'm really not in the mood to break out unappreciative jackholes. You feeling me?"

Petunia raised her hand. "Not ungrateful over here," she called out. "Just somewhat loose in the morals department and seriously vain."

"No worries," I told my cousin. "I've got your back."

"She's kind of rude," Rick muttered to me, clearly still put out about the wee-wee comment.

"She's completely and utterly socially unacceptable, but she's my cousin."

"Roger that," he said with a grin.

Gods, I adored him.

Walking over to Petunia's cell, I examined the lock. It was too bad we hadn't found keys, but at least the locks weren't secured with magic. Rick's fangs could take care of these babies in a hot sec. My wolf was very talented.

"So you want to explain yourself?" I asked, eyeing my voluptuous cousin.

"Not really," she said. "But I suppose I have to."

"Yep. Spit it out, cousin."

She sighed dramatically and tried to hide her mangled arm and hand from me. The thought of my flighty, beautiful cousin being tortured made my blood boil, but I stayed calm. It wouldn't do for me to blow up something and alert the Gnome army of our presence when we were so close to being out of here.

Petunia was proud. My pointing out that she wasn't her normal stunning self would not help matters. I just needed to get her out of here and safely home—not that she had one as far as I knew. Petunia usually went where the ocean breeze blew her. Clearly, that wasn't working out so great. After we got her out of here, she was going to plant her ass on the Mystical Isle for a while and let me and my sisters take care of her.

"Well, there was a secret party—or at least I thought there was," she said, shrugging her slim shoulders. "I wasn't invited, which was ridiculous. So I went. Due to my unfortunate need to socialize, I got kidnapped. End of story."

"Umm… there's a lot missing from that story." I rolled my eyes and grimaced. If she didn't want to tell me yet, that was fine. I'd get it out of her eventually.

"It wasn't a *party*," one of the more unpleasant lesser gods huffed rudely. He stared down his long pointy nose at us and tsked. "It was a set up for disaster."

"What do you mean?" Rick asked as his fangs dropped and he unlocked Petunia's cage and then bit through the chains that bound her and blocked her magic.

"Unacceptable," another lesser god hissed. "The cages of the gods will be opened before that of a *common Mermaid*. Lock her back up at once and release me."

"Is that fucker for real?" Rick growled, glancing over at me.

"'Fraid so," I told him with a shake of my head. "Lesser gods are dicks."

"You got that right," he said.

"I can't believe this," yet another rude lesser god commented condescendingly. "First he sets us up and then he sends a *swimming hooker* and a *wolf* to save us? What has the Universe come to?"

"Duuuude," I snarled as my fingers began to spit ominous pink sparks. "It would be in your best interests to shut your nasty cake hole. Now."

"Is she speaking to me?" he snapped, completely shocked. "Is that common Mermaid speaking that way to a *god*?"

Rick was done.

"Listen to me, you little smart-mouthed weenie nardhole. If you ever call my certifiably insane woman a swimming hooker again, I will shift and tear your innards out. I will then shove them into your ill-mannered mouth right before I rip your head from your shoulders. You feel me, dude?"

"Oookay, girlfriend," Petunia said with a wide smile. "Wee-wee man is soooooo hot."

"Right?" I said, tingling with pride. "He's hot and completely off his rocker. Perfect for me."

"You've got that right, cousin," Petunia said as she exited her cell and eyed the lesser gods with disgust. "You idiots have been bitching like teenage girls on the rag the entire time we've been here. Honestly, if the Gnomes hadn't been torturing me, I would have ripped my own gorgeous ears off my head to have some peace and quiet down here."

"Impertinent," a god muttered.

"Yep." She bowed to Rick in thanks and then turned her attention back to the lesser gods. "And I'm done with your small minded asses. You know," Petunia said with an evil little smirk. "I'd always thought gods were gifted in the junk department. Guess I was wrong."

"Ewwwww," I choked out with a gag. "You've been up close and personal with their junk?"

"They wish," Petunia said with a laugh and then sobered quickly. "No. Unfortunately, I've seen their less than stellar bits. The Gnomes strip us bare before torture—more humiliating that way."

"Speaking of Gnomes," Rick said tersely as he quickly and expertly unlocked all the cages, and then worked through the chains binding the lesser gods. "We need to haul ass out of here before today's torture time."

The gods huddled together and continued to insult us. I was ready to send a blast of magic and permanently shut their mannerless mouths for good, but that was not a great plan. Lesser gods were still gods—even though they defined the word dick.

"All right, boys," Rick said. "While you figure out how to say thank you, you should probably get your sorry asses out of here. Now. You should have enough power now that the chains are off."

"There is no need for us to thank *commoners*," the god with the unfortunate nose informed us. "It was your good fortune to get to save us."

Breathing in through my nose and out through my mouth, I visualized swimming in the crystal blue ocean while Rick ran on the beach and watched me. The picture in my mind calmed me. It would be a bad plan to exterminate the jacknards we'd been tasked to save—even though they deserved it.

"I'd like to suggest you poof on out of here," I said, narrowing my eyes dangerously as the crew. "The only reason you're still breathing is because Poseidon wants you back and I love the soused green haired weirdo."

"*Poseidon* is the reason we're here," one snarled. "He shall pay dearly for this folly."

Rick shook his head, pulled two wicked looking daggers from his belt, closed his eyes and threw them. The god was now pinned to the wall. It was so hot, I was tempted to jump him, but the timing was bad.

"Duuuude," he said to the dazed and shocked dummy. "If I were you, I wouldn't smack talk a guy who can get away with wearing a fucking diaper and somehow make it work."

"May I reiterate," Petunia said, clapping her hands. "The wee-wee wolf is seriously hot."

I nodded and grinned.

"You shall pay for that, along with the God of the Sea,"

another god shouted as they all disappeared in a cloud of musty blue smoke.

"Good riddance to bad rubbish," Petunia said, waving her hand to dissipate the icky smoke left in wake of their departure.

"What was that crap about Poseidon?"

"Who knows?" Petunia said with a shrug. "They babbled on and on how Poseidon set them up to be kidnapped. They're insane."

My eyes shot to Rick's in alarm and his narrowed in thought.

"You think they're telling the truth?" he asked, reaching back to make sure Neville was still okay.

"If they are, Poseidon has some 'splainin' to do," I said, darkly. "A whole *bunch* of 'splainin'."

"Well, there's no time like today to smack down on the God of the Sea," Rick said with a chuckle and a headshake. "You ladies ready to say goodbye to this joint?"

"You have no idea how much I'm ready to say goodbye," Petunia muttered as she walked toward the hallway to the exit. "I need a pedicure and to soak in some salt water."

Rick took my hand in his and grinned. "This was too easy."

"I know. Right? I guess playing it safe works sometimes," I said, patting Neville through the backpack. "Let's get you home to your mommy."

Famous last words... the explosive sound and the screams of agony made us liars.

Nothing worthwhile was ever *that* easy.

The time to play it safe was over.

18

RICK

FOR A BRIEF MOMENT, I CONSIDERED LEAVING THE BACKPACK behind. We were about to deal with Gnomes that were not the good kind. Keeping Neville strapped to my back was dangerous. However, leaving him behind could be deadly.

"Stay back here," Madison instructed Petunia as we sprinted past her towards the entrance of the dungeon.

"Tiny and Bart weren't armed," I growled, moving faster. "They won't stand a chance against one of the army Gnomes."

"Wouldn't have mattered," Madison said, producing wicked looking daggers from thin air and getting ready to use them. "They told me the weapons they carried when they greeted us were fake. The Undesirables aren't allowed to protect themselves."

"For fucking real?" I snarled and almost stopped in shock and fury. Only Madison's forward motion made me keep going.

The need to do some major damage consumed me. The hierarchy of the Gnome world was bullshit.

"Go for the nards. If we can incapacitate, I can behead them," I told her.

"Got it," she said with a curt nod. "Nards first. Heads next."

Putting my hand on her to slow her pace, we crouched low. The screaming had ceased. That never boded well.

"Stay against the wall," I whispered. "I'd bet my canines they're still there."

Nodding silently Madison plastered herself against the wall and we inched our way toward the iron door.

"On three... we go," she said softly, choking up on her daggers and checking the ones still in her belt.

Her eyes were lit with excitement and I knew mine matched. We were certifiable and insanely perfect for each other.

"Nards first," I mouthed with a small grin.

Holding up her fingers, she counted us down. It reminded me of our show, but this was far more real. Madison and I were nuts, but we never would have harmed each other. The thrill was the danger. This was far more than danger. This was potential death.

However, it wasn't going to be ours.

We had way too fucking much to live for.

Entrances were our forte and we made an excellent one. Not surprisingly, the audience wasn't thrilled to see us. Apparently, we weren't as famous with the *army* as we were with the Undesirables. However, we were outstanding at drawing the audience in and enjoyed it thoroughly. This show was no exception.

"Nards. Now," I growled as I cocked back to throw my knives at a few hairy midget sweet pickles flanked by two mini sets of peas.

The expressions on the faces of the Gnomes would have been funny if Tiny and Bart weren't lying dead at their feet. It looked as if Tiny's head was only attached by a few arteries and Bart was covered in so much green blood I couldn't even discern his head from the rest of his mutilated body.

The evil fuckers had worked fast. Of course, it helped tremendously that they were armed and Tiny and Bart were not.

Now the playing field was level.

The split-second hesitation from the four murderous Gnomes as they recognized us was all the time we needed. In perfect unison, Madison and I each hurled the daggers we carried.

And it perfect unison they hit their tiny hairy targets.

"Sweet Poseidon in gauchos," Madison gasped out as her mouth formed a perfect O. "You were right."

"Told ya so," I said as all four of the bastards curled into balls and began to scream like teenage girls at a Jonas Brothers' concert. "It lasts a half hour. I'm gonna shift and behead them."

"One of them is mine," Madison hissed. "For Tiny and Bart."

I nodded and began to remove my clothes. Laying the backpack gently on the floor, I shook my head. Neville was going to need a lot of love and a fucking therapist when we got him home. No child should be witness to any of this—

even one with the blood of a king and the blood of a god running through his veins.

"Keep your pecker covered, wee-wee wolf," Petunia ground out in a voice that was gods damned chilling as she walked through the door and examined the carnage. "All four are mine. These are my buddies. They had a play date with me every day for a month. Turnabout is fair play."

"Do you have enough power to do it?" Madison asked her cousin with concern. "Rick and I can take care of this. You've been through enough."

Petunia's eyes blazed red and her voice was hollow. "If you love me, you will let me do this. I need to do this."

Touching Madison's shoulder, I gently pulled her back. Vengeance rightly belonged to Petunia. And vengeance she would have.

"I love you," Madison said. "You do what you have to do."

"If I had the time I would use every spike, every torch, every whip, every blade and every ounce of searing hot boiling water that you used on me," she said calmly as the screaming Gnomes tried in vain to roll away from her. "But I'm much too good for that. I like to serve death swiftly and with class—something you wouldn't know about. You feel me?"

In the blink of an eye, Petunia beheaded all four Gnomes without even touching them. With a staccato clap of her hands, glimmering blood red magic swirled through the room and sliced right through the necks of the enormous Gnomes. Their heads rolled away and Petunia smiled.

"Didn't even break a nail," she said with a shrug.

"Remind me never to get on your cousin's bad side," I

muttered as Petunia kicked one of the rolling decapitated heads so hard it exploded.

"Will do," Madison said.

"Tiny and Bart not dead," Neville's muffled voice came from the far side of the room.

"Umm... not sure if you're aware of this," Petunia said, glancing back with a raised brow. "But your backpack can talk."

"Yep," Madison said as she knelt down and tried to access if Neville was correct about Tiny and Bart. "It's a very special backpack."

"It also wee-wees," I added, hoping she put two and two together and realized I hadn't wet my own pants. I didn't need Petunia to go back home and tell Madison's sisters that I needed a diaper.

Neville crawled out of the pack, toddled over and knelt down next to Madison. Petunia eyed the child with curiosity, but was smart enough not to ask questions.

"Neville, I think they're gone," Madison said, gently trying to pull him away.

"Nope. Me fix it," he said, patting Madison's hand to comfort her.

And I'll be damned if the little alien dude didn't do just that.

"Hold breath," Neville warned us with a giggle. "It be stinky."

With a wave of his chubby little hands, a cloud of noxious gold and green smoke filled the room. I see couldn't a thing, but I felt the enchantment—and it smelled like Hades on trash day in July. It was strong and felt warm as it feathered across my skin.

"Holy hell and seashells," Madison whispered as the smoke cleared.

A fully healed Tiny and Bart slowly sat up looking more shell shocked than we felt.

"Who are you?" Tiny asked, reaching out to touch Neville.

"Me Neville," he answered, crawling into the huge Gnome's lap and giving him a hug. "Me save you."

The two Gnomes looked at each other and began to cry. For big hairy dudes with deadly reputations, they certainly cried a lot. Gently putting Neville on the floor, Tiny and Bart got on their knees and bowed to the child.

"Salvation has come," Bart whispered. "The gods have been listening."

Their recognition of the rightful heir to the Gnome throne made my gut clench. It was beautifully terrifying. They were right and they were wrong. I didn't want to make them cry anymore because it smelled even worse than Neville's magic, but this shit wasn't going to fly just yet.

"Dudes," I said, scooping my little alien guy up and putting him into the backpack. "*Salvation* needs to grow up first. You know—go to school, play little league baseball, throw shit at cars, make prank phone calls to people he doesn't know, ride a rollercoaster naked, sneak into a Piggly Wiggly and rearrange all the food so the humans lose their shit the next time they shop, eat pop rocks and drink a Sprite, streak at a public event, jump off a..."

"Rick," Madison said, trying to bite back a grin. "Do you actually have a point here?"

I had to think about that for a second. "Yes. Neville has to leave before he can come back to stay. If King Stew was able to kill the little alien dude's father, he'll eat Neville for lunch. My little buddy is not ready for this shit yet and I'm not letting him stay here. Period. If anyone has a problem with that, they'll have to take it up with me." Crossing my arms over my chest and letting my fangs show, I eyed Tiny and Bart.

"Wee-wee wolf is going to be a great daddy someday," Petunia commented with a laugh. "A little unorthodox, but very good."

"Thank you," I said. The thought of having a mini Madison was amazing. The thought of a mini me was fucking terrifying. Hopefully, we'd only have girls.

"Welcome," she replied.

"Rick is right," Madison said, helping the enormous Gnomes to their feet. "We need to get Neville out of here. Tiny and Bart, will you help us do that?"

"Madison Diane with the bootylicious can and Jack Rick with the enormous dick, we would be humbled to help our savior escape," Bart said smiling so wide it was alarming.

"And we will wait anxiously for the day of his return," Tiny added, patting the backpack reverently. "You have given us hope."

"Great," I said, beginning to move. "If four of the army nards were on patrol down here, I'd bet my fangs more will come when the headless shits don't return. Let's haul ass."

And we did.

But it was too late.

Twenty vicious looking Gnomes blocked the entrance of the tunnel to freedom.

"I can't hit that many nards at the same time," Madison whispered as our small group jerked to a halt.

Accessing the incredibly shitty situation, I tried to figure out the odds of taking on all twenty. They sucked. "We go with them and pull a new plan out of our asses when the time is right."

"That's a dangerous plan," Petunia muttered.

"Danger is my middle name," I shot back under my breath.

"Wait. I thought your middle name was Rick," Tiny whispered, confused.

Madison's muffled giggle was music to my ears. The Mermaid was my world and if she could laugh in the face of danger that was potentially life ending so could I.

I closed my eyes for a second. However, if we made it out of this shit alive, I was going to consider playing it safe.

Nah, who was I kidding? Danger really should be my middle name. Jack Danger Rick with the enormous dick had a very nice ring to it.

19

MADISON

KING STEW'S CHAMBERS WERE AS GAUDY AND HORRIFYING AS the Gnome himself. The walls and floor were pure sparkling gold. Normally, as a Mermaid, I loved shiny things, but this was positively macabre. The bones of what I could only guess were Undesirables were embedded grotesquely into walls.

A large ornate throne sat atop a raised stage at the far end of the room. Chandeliers made of Gnome skulls hung from the vaulted ceilings. The repulsive kicker was that a rug of what appeared to be the fur of dead Gnomes lay under the throne, trimmed in blood encrusted fangs. The cavernous room had no windows so escape by taking a running leap and busting through the glass was looking grim.

As we waited for the arrival of the King, his army growled and hissed at us—gnashing fangs and all. For having no fear gene, I had to admit it was kind of terrifying.

"Think he's compensating for something?" Rick asked

casually, nodding his head at a huge portrait to the right of the throne.

It was all I could do not to shriek with laughter even though it felt like we were in one of the worst levels of Hell. I was so busy taking in the décor of bones I'd missed the life-sized painting of the evil ruler. The likeness was uncanny except for one teeny detail... in the junk area. King Stew's package had been *enhanced*. No midget sweet pickle and tiny peas for him. Nope, his Long John Silver and hush puppies were freakin' ginormous.

While the anatomically incorrect depiction of the King's twig and berries was amusing, the fact that we were surrounded by close to a hundred heavily armed Gnomes was not funny at all.

"Gnomes no like Air Supply," Neville whispered from the backpack.

"Umm... nobody likes living without an air supply," I muttered, glancing over at Rick in confusion.

"Thanks, little alien dude, but that's kind of a given," Rick said quietly. "Can't breathe? Can't live. Period."

"Nooo, silly Waaawuf. *Air Supply*," he insisted softly.

Everything Neville had told us so far was the truth. There had to be something to what he was telling us now.

"Can you be a little more specific?" I asked the passenger of the backpack quietly as I twisted my pink hair in my fingers and wondered if there was a trick to cutting off a Gnome's air supply. It couldn't be making the room smell bad. It smelled like fried butt already.

"Air Supply," Neville said again as the backpack shuddered on Rick's back. "Air Supply—a soft rock duo consisting of English singer-songwriter and guitarist

Graham Russell and lead vocalist Russell Hitchcock from Australia. Air Supply had many hits in the 1980s. They suck."

I was flabbergasted. I wasn't sure if it was because the Gnomes hated Air Supply or that Neville had spoken a sentence that didn't sound at all like a toddler.

"I love Air Supply," Rick said, completely insulted.

"They suck," Neville corrected him flatly.

I had to agree with Neville on this one. Rick was my perfect Werewolf in every way except for his taste in music. Whatever. The boinking was so stellar I could overlook his horrible love of crappy pop songs.

"They do *not* suck," Rick huffed. "*All Out of Love* used to be my anthem before I met Madison. Air Supply got me through some hard times. I styled my hair in the eighties just like the lead singer."

"You had an afro?" I asked with wide eyes and snort.

"I rocked it," Rick informed me.

"Sure you did," I muttered and then froze. The plan hatching in my head was bizarre, but it was worth a shot. "Do you remember any lyrics?"

"Of course I do," Rick said with an eye roll. "They're like poetry. I could recite every lyric they ever wrote right now."

"Gnomes hate Air Supply," Neville repeated.

The widest smile I'd ever produced pulled at my lips. The only smile that could beat mine, at that moment was Rick's.

"You ready to sing, Werewolf?" I asked.

"I'm tone deaf," Rick replied, suddenly nervous. "It could be dangerous for the future of our sex life if you hear me sing."

"Umm... *nothing* could be dangerous for the future of our sex life," I told him with a naughty grin. "The only thing that could end our sex life is if we don't make it out of the palace alive."

"Roger that," Rick said with a wink. "Prepare to be wowed by Air Supply."

"Here," Neville whispered as his little hand emerged cautiously out of the backpack and handed me two sets of earplugs.

"Dude, I'm not *that* bad of a singer," Rick said.

"Not for you, Waaawuf," Neville whispered with a giggle. "For Tiny and Bart so they live."

"Why do the Gnomes hate Air Supply so much?" I asked, taking the earplugs and covertly handing them to Bart and Tiny.

As they'd overheard the conversation, they quickly put them in.

"Because they suck," Neville said.

"Air Supply does *not* suck," Rick ground out through clenched teeth. "They're awesome."

Suddenly the atmosphere in the large chamber changed dramatically. It grew darker, colder and stinkier. The noxious stench was almost debilitating. I hoped someday if Neville became the Gnome King he would suggest better hygiene.

"And what have we here? Lunch?" King Stew roared in a bloodthirsty manner as he entered the chamber followed by ten emaciated Gnomes who crawled on all fours behind him.

They were definitely from the *Undesirable* population, but I found them far more *desirable* than the jackass they served.

The heinous King narrowed his beady eyes and licked

his fleshy lips. "I don't remember extending an invitation to *humans*."

My disgust for the Gnome King increased tenfold as he kicked one of the poor Undesirables and almost killed him just because he could. Not only was he evil, he was stupid. We were not human. Petunia was definitely not human. She'd been chained in his magic dungeon with the lesser gods for a freakin' month, for cryin' out loud.

"State your business before you die a slow and painful death," King Stew snarled, seating himself on his throne.

"Well, I was lying alone with my head on the phone. I was thinking of you till it hurt," Rick sang as a few of the guard Gnomes winced in agony and passed out.

Rick did not underestimate his singing skills at all. He was beyond tone deaf, he was *awful*. I was very happy we'd boinked before I'd heard him sing.

"WHAT?" the King hissed and slapped his hands over his ears.

"I know you hurt too," Rick said, giving the King a middle finger salute. "But what else can we do… tormented and torn apart."

"Tiny. Bart. When you can, move to the Gnomes at his feet and get them out of here. I don't want them hurt."

"Not problem," Neville whispered from the backpack. "How many?"

"Ten," I told him, hoping like heck he wasn't going to toddle on over and hand them earplugs. That would not end well.

"Look at them and me help, Mooomaid. Touch backpack," Neville said as I heard him clap his chunky little hands inside the backpack.

I obeyed the three-year-old without question. Touching the backpack, I concentrated on the beaten down group of Gnomes and didn't take my eyes off of them. The looks of grateful shock when they realized their ears were plugged made me wonder exactly how powerful Neville was. What he'd done so far was insane.

"Kill them," the King roared in a fury to his army. "Skin the humans alive and bring me their heads. NOW!"

"I wish I could carry your smile in my heart," Rick sang in the key of Z at the top of his lungs as the army shrieked in terror and began to explode into steaming piles of thick green goop.

"Keep going," I shouted, pulling knives and aiming for the hairy sweet pickles. If the singing didn't get them, a knife to the nards would at least slow them down and give us a chance to get Neville out of here.

Petunia joined me and laughed like a Mermaid who'd ingested too much seaweed. "I haven't had this much fun in centuries," she squealed, lobbing machetes at the charging Gnome's furry jewels.

"You really need to get out more if you think this is fun," I said with an eye roll. It was no surprise that my cousin used machetes instead of knives. She'd always been a bit over the top.

"What would you say if I called on you now... said that I can't hold on," Rick continued while also throwing knives and dancing around to keep Neville safe.

Tiny and Bart were basically glued to Rick's back. Protecting their savior was serious business. Realizing they were still defenseless, I conjured up some explosives and handed them off to the boys while still hurling daggers with my teeth. I'd perfected that skill in show seven of *Bitchin' in the Kitchen*. Rick had been wildly impressed. The boys gave me a thankful thumbs up and began lobbing bombs at what was left of the raging army.

Everything was going great… until it wasn't.

How in the heck could I have forgotten about Kim and Bonar? It was very clear they'd received the text. However, the timing of their arrival couldn't have been shittier. They poofed right into the chambers and were greeted with flying knives and exploding Gnomes. Thankfully, they landed next to us and not in the middle of the Gnomes who were trying to kill us. I knew Bonar would be fine—he was a freakin' Sphinx. But without Kim knowing what she was, there was no way she could fight her way out of anything going on in here.

"Oh my gods," Kim screamed as she took in the war raging around us. "Does he have him?"

"Yes," I said. "He's in the backpack."

The fact that neither of us had used *names* to clarify who we were talking about was a fatal fucking mistake that would give me nightmares the rest of my immortal life.

"He dies," Kim shouted as she took off like a bullet out of a gun and headed straight for the Gnome King. "He murdered Dirk. He will *not* murder our son."

"*What the fuck?*" Rick shouted over the screaming and in between the lyrics of the song. "What is she doing?"

"Don't ask," I yelled back as I conjured up more knives and prepared to go after her. "Just keep singing."

"Nay," Bonar snarled as smoke and fire flamed out of every orifice on his body. "I will rescue me love."

My wildly inappropriate mind went to the worst possible

scenario at the worst possible time. I was curious if Bonar's butthole shot fire too. Thankfully, I was able to overcome my nosy need for information that wasn't in the least bit relevant at the moment. I'd simply ask him later if we made it out of here alive.

"NO," Neville shouted, popping his upper body out of the backpack and grabbing Bonar's puffy shirt in a vise-like grip. "Me save me mommy. Is the way it supposed to be. Me daddy tell me so."

"Shit," Rick growled. "He's *three*. Not sure this is a good plan."

I agreed and then was stunned to silence in a big fat hairy way. Everyone was. Especially the King.

Rick's strong body was forced to the ground as Neville's body burst from the backpack and grew in size to the point I thought his head might hit the twenty-foot ceilings. The army Gnomes who weren't already gobs of goop on the ground, shrank back in terror and tried to run from the chamber.

Neville didn't like that and waved his hand. Every single living member of the Gnome army was now trapped in a cage and chained within an inch of their lives.

"Shit," Rick muttered as he got to his feet and scanned the room. "We should have let our alien dude out of the bag sooner. Would have saved some time. The little shit is fucking good."

"Right?" I whispered, craning my neck back to take in all of little Neville who was no longer *little*.

"You will do nothing," King Stew screamed maniacally as he held Kim by her throat with one hand and a razor-sharp knife in the other. "If you take one step toward me, the whore who bore you will die, you abomination."

"Me no move, bad man," Neville said with a shrug.

Neville's voice was deeper. He sounded like a thug toddler with a massive head cold. Neville stood around twenty feet high and was the largest freakin' Gnome I'd ever seen. However, the amazing part was that he didn't smell bad. He still smelled like a sweet little boy.

"This is a bad idea," Rick whispered. "I think we're about to watch Kim bite it."

"Nay," Bonar said tersely as he held himself back with effort. "Listen to the words the wee bairn uses."

Neville was not a wee bairn by any stretch of the imagination. But I supposed that to Bonar, Neville would always be a baby.

"He said he wouldn't move," I hissed. "If he doesn't move, Kim dies."

"Watch," Bonar whispered. "Just watch."

Never have I been so happy to be wrong in my three hundred years...

"Me think you should put me mommy down," Neville said calmly.

His deep voice made the room tremble. The King should have noticed this, but a narcissist assnard is only aware of himself.

"Go back to your human form and come and kneel to your King. If you do, the whore will live," King Stew sneered, knowing he'd won.

"Me mommy not whore," Neville corrected the King politely. "And if you push knife in, me will end you slow. If you drop mommy now, me will end you quick."

"YOU WILL NOT END ME," the King screamed as his face went so red, I thought his brains might pop out. "I am the Gnome King. You are nothing but a worthless mutt—a half breed. Part human scum."

"You wrong," Neville said with a giggle.

The giggle was weird coming out of something the size of a house, but it was one hundred percent Neville.

"Me part Gnome and part god. You is scum," Neville said in a growly voice. "You kill me daddy and you hurt me people. You is done."

"NEVER," King Stew hissed as spittle flew from his mouth and covered his face.

As the King raised his arm high with the dagger in it, Neville again waved his hand. However, this time his wave caused a strong breeze to rip through the room. Grabbing onto Rick and Bonar so I didn't blow away, I watched in awe as the enchanted wind wrapped Kim in a loving embrace and pulled her from the Gnome King's deadly embrace.

"Me people," Neville commanded the wind.

The wind did his bidding.

Gently lifting the prone undesirables from the ground, the magical breeze brought them to the ginormous feet of their savior. Neville bent down and gently patted their heads.

"You be okay now. Me promise," he told them and then stood back up to his full height. "Come to me, mommy."

Still wrapped in the wind, Kim floated to her beloved son and threw herself at him. She only came up to his hairy knee, but the love was abundantly obvious.

"Care for me mommy, Booonar. Me not done here."

With a nod of delighted approval, Bonar shielded Kim in

his arms. "Would be honored, me matey," Bonar replied.

The story of the demise of the evil Gnome King would be passed down through many generations. The story would grow with time and exaggeration, but the real version was pretty damned good.

In a fit of rage and an accurate idea that his mortality was in serious jeopardy, the Gnome King made a run for it. Neville had been correct about not needing to move to save his beloved mommy. However, he had made no promises about moving to end the tyrant that had tried to destroy his race. But as the story goes, he only had to move a little.

As the King sprinted from the room on that fated day, Neville took one giant step—just one. That was all he needed to take since he was over a hundred feet tall—*according to the exaggerated version of the story.*

In his haste to escape, the King hadn't even seen it coming. He was too consumed with his own life to see the dark shadow in the shape of a massive Gnome foot hovering over his head. And when he did it was too late.

With a toddler's giggle and a sickeningly loud crunch, the savior of the Gnomes stepped on the villainous bastard. The evil King was crunched to a gooey pile of gunk under the foot of his very own grandson.

Karma was a bitch and best served without much movement—just ask Neville.

But the best part of the story—and this part was always the same no matter who was relaying it—was the comment from the brave and very handsome Werewolf, better known as Jack Rick with the enormous dick. His shouted exclamation of, *"Motherfucker, that had to hurt,"* was now the bestselling t-shirt in the land.

20

RICK

"*MOTHERFUCKER, THAT HAD TO HURT,*" I SHOUTED AS THE EVIL assnard of a King was crunched to death by a foot that had to wear at least a size 100 shoe.

"Holy hell and seashells," Madison grunted with a wince as Neville stepped back and examined the results. "That was gnarly."

"Understatement," I added with an impressed shake of my head.

"Me done now," Neville said with a giggle as he morphed back to his little alien dude size.

Kim wrapped her child in her arms and kissed his face all over. "I love you so much," she said, glaring at the smiling toddler. "I will let this one slide, but I do not *ever* want to hear about you stepping on people again. And no stowing away in cars. Am I clear?"

"Yep," he said, yawning. "Me tired."

"Me too," Poseidon bellowed as he poofed in on the scene about an hour or two or ten too late.

Madison marched right over to the God of the Sea and whacked him in the head. "Well, if it isn't the diaper wearing buttdong. You have some explaining to do."

"What did you just call me?" Poseidon demanded, squinting at my Mermaid.

"A diaper wearing buttdong," I volunteered, quickly stepping in front of Madison to take any wrath that the soused old fart decided to dish out. He wasn't going to zap my gal. Ever. If he tried I would shove his diaper so far up his arse, it would get stuck in his throat. "And she's correct. You have some serious explaining to do."

Poseidon laughed like the loon that he was and scanned the room. Walking over to the gooey remains of King Stew, he nodded with satisfaction. "Job well done."

"Grand Pappy!" Neville shouted joyously as he slid out of his mother's embrace and charged over to the green haired dumbass. "Me is Neville!"

"Oh, I know who you are," Poseidon said, lifting the child into his arms and hugging him close. "It's nice to meet you in person finally."

"You forgot your clothes," Neville pointed out with a giggle.

As usual, the god was sporting only a diaper.

"Aye, that I did," Poseidon said, delighted with the child.

"What's going on here?" Kim demanded, narrowing her eyes dangerously at Poseidon. "You're the one from my dreams. What do you want with my son?"

"My great-great-great-great-great-great-great-great-great-great-great-great-great-great-great-great-great-great-great-grandson," Poseidon corrected a shocked Kim. "Which makes you a descendant of mine as well, young lady."

And, at that bizarre piece of news, Kim promptly passed out cold. Bonar held his love in his arms and nodded to Poseidon. Kim could get caught up on her colorful history when she woke up. Right now, it was the soused God of the Sea's turn to spill it.

"Did you get your lesser gods back?" I questioned, watching his reactions carefully.

"Aye, I did," he replied, studying his fingernails. "Thank you for that. Those dicks are home and no worse for the wear. All's well that ends well."

"Nope," Madison snapped. "Not buying it. You set them up to be kidnapped. Didn't you?"

Poseidon lifted a bushy green brow as a smirk formed on his lips.

"Well, that certainly sucks since I got caught up in the bullshit," Petunia commented, flipping a surprised Poseidon off.

"This piece of information I didn't know," Poseidon said, sounding less drunk than I'd ever heard him. He crossed to Petunia and patted her head lovingly. "I'm sorry, child. If I had known, I would have retrieved you."

Petunia nodded her head and sighed. "Serves me right for crashing a party."

"Where do you reside now?" he questioned.

"On the Mystical Isle," Madison butted in, giving her cousin the eyeball and daring her to argue. "She is coming home with me... and Rick."

"Interesting," Poseidon said with a wide grin. "Thought neither of you daredevils were in the market for a keeper."

"You're avoiding questions, old man," I said.

"Thought you wouldn't notice that," he said with a

chuckle, pulling a bottle of rum from his diaper and throwing back a healthy swig. "Anyone?" he asked, offering up his booze.

No one took him up on it since it had been hanging out with his balls for gods only knew how long.

"More for me," he said, taking another swig. "So ask your questions. I'm in a chatty mood."

"You had those dicks kidnapped?" Madison repeated.

"If you're referring to the lesser gods, then yes," he replied, cagily.

"And you knew Kim worked on *Bitchin' in the Kitchen'*?" I demanded, still not clear on why he done all he'd done.

"Of course, I had her hired."

"The bar you sent us to?" I asked. "You knew the Gnomes and Kim would be there?"

"Yep."

"Did you have the show canceled?" Madison asked, perplexed.

"Gods no," Poseidon said. "You two did that one all on your own."

"Makes sense," I muttered.

"It really does," Madison said with a giggle.

Taking her hand in mine, I glared at Poseidon. "And the Gnome King?" I pressed, thinking about how we all could have bitten the dust. I liked living on the edge, but only the edge. "You wanted him dead?"

"Didn't we all?" Poseidon shot back.

"Then why didn't you just do it?" Madison hissed. "You created a freakin' shit show of almost deadly proportions by meddling in everyone's lives."

"Because I couldn't," Poseidon bellowed. "I'm not

permitted to interfere in the lives of species not under my jurisdiction. Breaking the Laws of Nature come with jail time in Hades and stiff fines. And there is no rum in prison," he added with a shudder and took another belt off the bottle.

"Could have fooled me. I'm not in your jurisdiction," I said. I was a Werewolf not an ocean creature.

"You owed me," he pointed out victoriously. "Therefore I had the gods' given right to mess with you."

"Didn't owe you. Already repaid my debt," I reminded him.

"Shit. You're right. My bad," Poseidon said with a large grin. "Are you unhappy that I messed with you, boy?"

Damn it. He had me there. I wasn't mad at all. Not about any of it. Madison was the greatest thing to happen to me in my very long and lonely life. I would do everything again and then some to have won her love.

"Hold your seahorses. You set Rick and me up to fall in love?" Madison shouted.

"I definitely set you up," Poseidon said, still grinning from ear to ear. "I was only *hoping* the two most certifiably insane people I've ever come across would fall in love."

"That's certainly an interesting comment coming from you, considering you're batshit crazy," Petunia pointed out.

"You don't know Rick yet," Madison said with pride, squeezing my hand. "My Werewolf makes the diaper wearing buttdong look sane."

"Thank you," I told the love of my life. "And you're the most beautiful certifiably crazy assed woman I've ever met."

"Isn't he the bomb?" Madison gushed. "And we stab each other too."

"Umm… not going to touch that one," Petunia said as she grabbed Poseidon's rum and drank the rest of the bottle. Guess she didn't care about a little ball sweat.

"So if we're done with the interrogation, I say we take this party outside. Smells like Zeus' ass on a Thursday in here—the idiot only bathes on Fridays," Poseidon explained.

"Not so fast," I said with a slight gag. "Why? I still don't know why you did everything. And PS, that was TMI about Zeus."

"My bad," he said contritely.

"No worries. Just don't want to hear about the gods' hygiene, or lack thereof. Makes my gag reflex kick in," I replied. "Keep talking, you old fart."

"Do I have to explain everything?" the god asked with an enormous eye roll.

"YES," everyone in the room shouted.

"Fine," Poseidon pouted and pulled another bottle of rum from his man diaper. "Quite some time ago, back when gods boinking humans was all the rage, I met and mated with a lovely woman. Kim is from that line."

"Oookkaaay," Madison said. "You boinked a human. We got that part. You've boinked a lot. You have over nine hundred children." Madison froze and blanched. "Sweet hell and slimy seashells, Kim is related to Pirate Doug. She's gonna shit."

"Who's Pirate Doug?" I asked.

"The nard my sister married."

"That nard is also my son," Poseidon added with a nod of agreement at the assessment his offspring was a nard. "Anyhoo, Neville's life was in danger and it was time to end the suffering of the Gnome race. Normally, we leave the leadership of species up to the species themselves. However, once Stew offed his son, we figured it was fair game to step in."

"How did you end up in charge of this particular shit show?" I asked, knowing there was more—there was always more with Poseidon. "Did you lose at strip poker?"

"Good guess, boy," he said with a laugh. "But no. I took this one on personally since my own flesh and blood was involved. I see this as a grand slam in the bottom of the ninth. Neville and Kim are safe. You and Madison are in love. King Stew is dead and the Gnomes can live in peace until Neville is of age to rule them."

"Who will rule the Gnomes until Neville grows up?" Madison asked.

"That's a fine question, my little pink-haired daredevil," Poseidon said. He turned to Neville who was cuddled happily in Tiny's hairy arms. "Who do you choose to rule in your stead until the time is right for you to take your rightful throne?"

Neville smiled sleepily at Poseidon. "Me choose Tiny and Bart to rule while me grow up. And me also wear diaper when me become the Gnome King."

Poseidon's bellow of laughter filled the chamber. "Excellent choice of proxy and outstanding choice of fashion. You will be a fine leader someday. *Nooowwww* are we ready to take this party outside?"

"We are," I said, pulling Madison close to my side. "It's time to go home. Home where we belong."

21

MADISON

"Wow," I said, watching the *Undesirables* sing and dance with joy so pure my eyes watered. They were not undesirable. They never were. The most undesirable one of all was now a pile of goo. Poseidon's methods sucked all kinds of butt, but the end results were stellar.

As Tiny and Bart relayed the story, hundreds of Gnomes went to their knees and bowed to Neville. The plan for Tiny and Bart to rule for a while until Neville grew up was accepted with shouts of delight. After a prolonged and reverent bow, the party started again. It was kind of stinky since all the Gnomes enjoyed dancing with their arms in the air, but at this point I was getting used to it. Their happiness outweighed my need for unpolluted air by a long shot.

"This is great," Rick shouted, swinging me around. "Bonar said that a Pirate called Upton is watching over the animals in his absence and would be happy to sail my zoo to the Mystical Isle. Isn't that fucking awesome?"

"Yes," I squealed, planting a kiss on the lips of the man

that was going to make eternity a whole lot more fun.
"Guess what I did?" My stomach tingled and my smile was
so wide that it hurt my mouth.

"What did you do, Mermaid?" he asked, tilting his head
and grinning.

"I made reservations for us to go blowhole diving in
Hawaii, Werewolf," I announced as his eyes lit up like
fireworks.

"I love you."

"I love you more," I said with a laugh.

"Not possible," Rick said, growing serious. "That's not
possible."

Before I could argue the point, Poseidon tapped Rick on
the shoulder. "Some people are here to see you, boy."

"Who?" he asked, turning his head to see.

His body tensed and he held me so tight I thought I
might break. Slowly releasing me as if he forgot I was there,
he left me with Poseidon and warily approached the fifty
people waiting for an audience with him. I knew
immediately it was his pack. The man in front was a dead
ringer for my Werewolf.

"Rob," Rick said, flatly.

"Rick," Rob said, eyeing his brother. "We have come to
offer an olive branch."

"I don't really like olives much," Rick replied.

All the Gnomes halted their revelry and watched the
unfolding drama. Jack Rick with the enormous dick was
very beloved in this community. He was a rock star of sorts.
If anyone fucked with him—even his own kind—the
Gnomes were not gonna have it.

"Always have to have the last word," Rob said, extending his hand to his brother.

It seemed like an eternity before Rick took his brother's hand, but as he did Rob pulled him into an embrace and held him tight.

"Is that his brother?" Poseidon asked quietly, offering me some rum.

I nodded and took the bottle. My throat was so choked with emotion, I didn't care that the bottle probably had ball sweat on it. I needed a hit of something strong so I didn't cry. I couldn't imagine my life without my sisters. Seeing Rick with his brother made my insides wonky. Family was everything.

"We are proud of what you have done here and want to welcome you back into the pack," Rob said, drawing back but keeping a hand on his Rick. "What do you say?"

Rick said nothing. He continued to stare at his brother. From my vantage point I couldn't see Rick's face, but I could only imagine his happiness. If my sisters had banished me and then wanted me back, I would go willingly. My stomach continued to churn and I felt lightheaded.

"I'll be retiring soon and the honor of being Alpha shall be yours."

Still, Rick said nothing. Why didn't he say something? Why didn't he tell them about me?

"And to show that we are of true intention, we have brought your mate with us. She is ready and willing to be yours."

A gorgeous blonde haired woman approached Rick and knelt at his feet. My stomach now felt like it had been punched so hard it would never recover. Turning and running to the very same Mulberry tree we'd hidden under earlier, I let the tears flow. I needed the ocean. I would die without it. My sisters were my anchor and without them, I would float out to sea and be lost forever. Did Rick need his own kind as well? What kind of horrible selfish Mermaid was I to be happy that he was going to leave his world behind to join mine?

"Madison?" Poseidon said, peeking through the leaves.

I almost laughed. The leaves matched his hair and he looked ridiculous. But the giggle got stuck in my throat.

"Tell me what's wrong, child."

"I love him," I whispered.

"That doesn't seem to be a problem," he said, coming under the tree with me and again offering me rum.

Alcohol would not dull the horrible pain I was feeling. Plus it was insanely difficult for an immortal to get drunk. Poseidon was an anomaly.

"I offered to stay here with him and live in the woods," I said, starting to blubber.

"And?"

"He said he wanted to live on the island with me for a few centuries."

"Still not seeing a problem here," Poseidon stated, confused.

"He has a mate waiting for him—a Werewolf mate—a *beautiful* Werewolf mate. He won't have to worry about having a hairy fish with claws and fangs."

Poseidon choked in his rum and stared at me. "A what?" he asked, alarmed.

"A hairy fish with claws and fangs," I repeated as the tears came faster. "He would have beautiful little Werewolf babies that looked like him. And they want him to be Alpha. That's a *really* big deal. Even I know that."

"Let me tell you something," Poseidon said with a shake of his head. "Being in charge is not all it's cracked up to be. The paperwork alone is gas inducing."

"You are not helping me," I hissed.

"My bad," he said, backing up a bit.

I'd nailed him pretty hard earlier. I didn't blame him.

"How about this," Poseidon suggested. "You go out there and offer to kick his fake mate's ass and tell those Lupine assholes that Rick is moving to the Mystical Isle with you."

"That's the worst idea I've ever heard," I snapped and then started a new round of sobbing. "I love him."

"So what are you going to do?" he asked, patting my head like I was a dog and trying to comfort me.

It didn't work, but the sentiment was appreciated.

"I'm going to leave," I whispered as my heart broke into a million tiny pieces.

"Call me crazy," he said.

"Crazy," I replied.

"I wasn't finished," Poseidon said with an eye roll.

"Sorry—my bad."

"I should say so," he muttered. "If you love the idiot, why are you leaving?"

"Because I love him that much. I can't take him away from his rightful destiny. If I go, he won't have to make a decision. He'll stay and be where he's meant to rule. He'll have a happy life with his people."

"I see a lot of holes in that plan," Poseidon said.

"You're drunk," I told him.

"Your point?" he asked, not following.

"Please send me home, Poseidon," I begged. "I want to go home now."

"I think you're making a mistake here, little Mermaid."

I thought over what Poseidon had just said. Occasionally he made sense. Right now, he didn't. He had no clue how much I loved Rick and what I would sacrifice for that love. Doing the right thing was killing my soul, but taking Rick away from his world would destroy his. I would not do that. Ever. I would live out eternity on the Mystical Isle. Alone. I idly wondered for a second if a Mermaid had ever become a nun. I'd have to research that.

"I want to go home," I told Poseidon.

"Are you sure?"

I nodded my head so I wouldn't fall apart.

"As you wish, little Mermaid. "As you wish."

EPILOGUE

MADISON

"JUST ANOTHER FREAKIN' DAY IN PARADISE," I MUTTERED TO NO one as I dipped back down under a crashing wave.

Swimming in the deep crystal blue ocean with schools of brightly colored fish used to calm my soul and make me feel alive. Now it left me feeling empty and sad. I'd been crying for the entire ten hours since I'd been home and Tallulah had finally ordered me to go for a long swim. She was certain it would help.

She was wrong.

My heart was shattered, but thankfully several lovely things had happened. The minute Kim, Neville and Bonar had arrived, Kim's tail showed up. It was a lovely orange-red with some flecks of green. Of course, she freaked out, downed half a bottle of antacids and then fainted, but when she came around Bonar and Neville had joined her for her first dip in the sea as a Mermaid. It would be difficult to keep Kim conscious long enough to hear the new information she was going to have to take in, but Bonar would be right at her side.

Neville was a huge hit with everyone, which was no surprise at all. Pirate Doug was beside himself that Neville was his blood relative. He immediately dressed the little guy in a puffy shirt, breeches and boots.

Rick would have gotten a kick out of seeing his little alien dude dressed that way, but I wasn't going to think about Rick other than to wish him all the happiness in the Universe. I would have to find my own happiness knowing that he was fulfilling his destiny. It sucked, but it was right. I'd even purchased Air Supply's greatest hits on my phone during a particularly epic crying fit. I was going to adopt Rick's old anthem. *I'm All Out of Love* fit me well now.

And horror of all horrors, it turned out that Pirate Doug loved Air Supply too. It made me sad to think how much fun he and Rick would have had starting a tribute band. They would have sucked all kinds of ass since Rick was tone deaf and people literally blew up when Pirate Doug sang, but they would have had such a good time.

Neville still thought Air Supply sucked, but he was a Gnome and that was a given. I was sure Neville was wearing pilfered clothes from *Uncle Pirate Doug*, but the little guy's joy of being an honorary Pirate stopped me from asking where Pirate Doug had *procured* the outfit.

Kim was wildly alarmed by her new relation, Pirate Doug and did her best to keep a straight face as he regaled her with his adventures of stealing lawn furniture from Target. She had gone from a family of two to a family of many. I couldn't wait for her to meet Rickety Shelia Clotlegs the Sea Hag. Rickety Shelia was another freakish spawn of Poseidon's. It could take Kim a century to meet all of Poseidon's offspring. She was going to need a lot of antacids.

Petunia had been strangely quiet upon her arrival, but I knew she would come around. With the love and attention my sisters were already lavishing on her, she would be fine. Finding her was one of the best parts of my adventure. She was lost and now she was found.

Poking my head above the water, I frowned and glanced around. I had a weird feeling of déjà vu. My heart was broken and I couldn't shake the unrest in my soul. I hoped Tallulah was right. Maybe I could swim my cares away.

Doubtful, but I was going to try.

The icy cold water on my overheated skin no longer calmed me. Weaving in and out of the waves, I let my tail do most of the work. White foamy caps on the waves burst and slid back into the sea, morphing to a clear teal blue. The feeling of gliding through the salty water only made me remember the aquarium in Tennessee. The restlessness of the sea creatures and imagining my life without my Werewolf made my swimming almost manic. Moving fast enough was impossible. And I wasn't sure if I was swimming toward my own personal hell or away. Something strange, or bad, or weird was going to happen... or possibly strange, bad *and* weird. Kind of like my shitty luck lately.

I supposed I could ask Poseidon to send me on another mission, but the thought was depressing.

I would just swim. I would swim all the oceans in succession. That should take a few months or years. I would tell my sisters I needed some alone time. I knew a few

ROBYN PETERMAN

dolphins that might be up for a marathon swim. They didn't actually speak, but that meant they couldn't ask questions. Right now, I didn't want to talk. And I was far too busy crying to actually make any sense anyway.

Closing my eyes and letting the currents take me where they chose. I sighed. I would miss Rick for all eternity. And Poseidon's words haunted me.

Had I made a mistake?

No.

I loved Rick with all my heart. It would have been wrong to take him away from his brother and his pack. However, the thought of his blonde mate made me ill.

I would never love another. Never.

"Motherhumpin' Chicken of the Sea," I grunted as my eyes popped open to see what my head had bashed into. Even the currents weren't on my side today. "What the heck?"

My head had connected with wood—the wooden hull of a ship. What in the Seven Seas was a ship doing in the area? It was Friday. The cruise ships came in on Mondays. Unless Pirate Doug had taken our new friends on a sail, there was someone in our waters who shouldn't be there.

No one was allowed in the waters around the Mystical Isle without permission. No one.

I swam to the surface to give whoever it was a piece of my mind and possibly a zap in the ass for being in my way. Just as I was about to let the boater have it, I gasped in shock. My body began to tingle and my never-ending supply of tears took over.

"I was wondering if you knew the way to the Mystical Isle?" the most beautiful man in the Universe inquired as he stood on deck with a raccoon on his head and a bunch of doggies and kitties at his feet.

I was too tear clogged to find my voice. Thankfully, Rick had no problem finding his.

"You see, I'm looking for a Mermaid. Her name is Madison Diane with the bootylicious can. Maybe you know her," he said, pinning me with a stare that made me feel light headed. "She told me that she loved me and would never leave me... but then she did. She's also supposed to take me blowhole diving in Hawaii. I love blowhole diving. Have you ever been?" he asked with a twinkle in his bright blue eyes.

Still unsure of my voice, I nodded.

"Here's the funny thing," Rick said, leaning over the rail of the ship and grabbing me under my arms.

He heaved me up, put my soaking wet body on his lap and held me tight. My tail twitched with delight and Thor, the skinny pit bull, wandered over and laid his head on my shoulder.

"So as I was saying," Rick continued, gently pushing my wet hair out of my face. "I heard a rumor from a nutjob wearing a diaper that she left so that I could fulfill my *destiny*—you know become the Alpha, mate with a woman I don't even know and have no desire to mate with."

"She was really pretty," I whispered and then hid my face against his massive chest.

Putting two fingers under my chin, he lifted my face so our eyes met and locked. "I didn't notice," he said. "I only have eyes for one woman. The woman who loves the real me, and that's *you*. You are my destiny."

"They want you to be the *Alpha*," I protested, needing to kiss him more than I wanted to take my next breath.

"I'd rather get a nine-to-five," he said with a laugh. "And if you had stayed just a bit longer you would have heard me tell my brother to shove the Alpha job up his ass—too much paperwork for me. I'm much happier scaling buildings, riding motorcycles blindfolded and getting stabbed in the ass by a sexy mermaid with pink hair than I would be leading a bunch of carnivores who think I'm an idiot with a death wish."

"For real?" I asked with a tiny smile starting to pull at my lips.

"Yep. And you would have gotten a real kick out of this part. I told all of them in no uncertain terms that I would not mate with anyone except the woman who could see me—the real me. The one who liked what she saw even with all the flaws. However, when I called to her to come meet my pack she was gone."

"Oh my gods," I said, hiding my face again in his chest. "I'm so sorry."

"Nah, it was funny. My brother thinks I'm making you up—called you Miss Snuffleupagus," he said with a laugh. "After I kicked his ass for saying that, we decided to let bygones be bygones."

"He's your brother," I said, feeling so at home in Rick's strong arms. "You should keep in touch."

"Madison, what I have with my brother is not like what you have with your sisters," he said, pressing his forehead to mine. "Sometimes you get lucky with your family. And sometimes you don't."

"I'm sorry," I said, tracing his full lips with my finger. Rick grinned. "I'm not. Families don't have to be blood-related, baby. If your family doesn't want you, you create your own. You're my family now. And if you ever run off like that again without talking to me first, I'm gonna have to sing Air Supply songs to you nonstop for three weeks."

"One week," I bargained with a laugh—a real laugh full of joy.

"Two weeks and you have yourself a deal and some bloody eardrums."

"I'll take it," I whispered against his mouth. "How's your Johnson doing?"

"He would very much like to get reacquainted with you. However, you have to promise me something."

What's that?"

"Next time you want to do something for my own good, I need you to talk to me first. You feel me?"

My grin widened and I reached down low. "I feel you and you feel damned good, Werewolf," I said and then sobered at the enormity of what was happening. Cupping his face in my hands, I stared right into the depths of his bright blue eyes. "I'm so sorry. I thought I was doing the right thing. I love you. Do you want to stab me in the butt? I deserve it."

"Nope, you did what you thought was right—but you were wrong. The *right thing* is breaking animals out of high kill shelters. The *right thing* was making sure my little alien dude survived his stowaway road trip. The *right thing* was not drinking Poseidon's rum because he stores it by his nards. You catching my drift here?"

"I am," I said with a giggle.

"And the wrong thing is to run from the person who makes you whole—who loves you completely. Forever," he said, lifting me up and carrying me to the cabin on the ship. "You might want to lose the tail for a week. We've got some unfinished business to take care of."

"A week?"

"A week," he confirmed with a lopsided grin that made my heart skip a beat. "Once I bite you, we're gonna boink for a while."

"A *week*?" I repeated myself. "You can go for a week?"

"I'm a Werewolf, baby. And you're my Mermaid. I can go for the rest of my life as long as you're in my arms."

And the man wasn't lying. We spent a week on the boat boinking until neither of us could see straight. Upton came and picked up the menagerie so they could have some shore leave. My sisters quietly delivered food while we were indisposed which was lovely of them... kind of. I knew they just wanted to check out my man and give me shit. I accepted it gracefully and Rick charmed them to the max during one of our boink breaks.

Life was so good.

I knew Rick and I would never play it *safe*. But dangerous on my own had lost its appeal. Without a partner in crime, life just wasn't as much fun. I hadn't known what I was missing until the insane Werewolf blasted into my life. And I thank the gods he did—most specifically, Poseidon. If it wasn't for the wasted diaper-wearer playing matchmaker I would be alone.

Maybe we would get married. I mean, how much worse

than Tallulah's wedding could mine be? There was only one way to find out.

Mrs. Jack Rick with the enormous dick did have a nice ring to it.

— The End... for now —

Want to hear about my new releases?
Visit robynpeterman.com and join my mailing list!

READ THE NEXT BOOK IN THE SERIES! PETUNIA'S PANDEMONIUM

SEA SHENANIGANS, BOOK 5

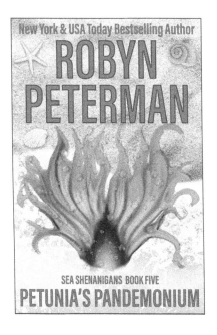

Go here for more info!

And read on for the blurb.

PETUNIA'S PANDEMONIUM

Mix one part Mermaid—one part Genie. Throw in an intoxicated God of the Sea and and a few smack-talking Pirates. What have you got?
Pandemonium.
Petunia's Pandemonium to be more accurate.

Petunia
Letting the ocean current take me where it may for the last twenty-five years hasn't worked out so great. So, instead of getting my tail in a knot, I'm making some swimmingly simple changes.
—Stay on Mystical Isle with my cousins who love me.
—Avenge my parents and eliminate the sea monster who's wreaking havoc.
—Forget about the gorgeous, no-good Genie who left me at the altar… so to speak.
—Stay away from Genies until the end of time.

—Join Poseidon's embarrassingly named online dating service for Immortals and get back into the game.

What could go wrong?

Del

I'm a Genie in a bottle baby. Or at least I was. After spending a quarter of a century, doing time for streaking at the Super Bowl after being destroyed by love, I'm a free man. It's time to get my life together and forget about the Mermaid who didn't want me. The list is simple.

—Stop granting wishes to idiots.

—Figure out why the Genie Star Fire Light in my eyes is burning out before I die a slow agonizing death.

—Eat an outstanding cheeseburger.

—Stay away from Mermaids.

—Join Poseidon's embarrassingly named online dating service for Immortals and get back into the game.

It's a plan. Not necessarily a stellar one, but it's a plan.

Come for the Vacation. Stay for the Shenanigans!

Go here for more info!

ROBYN'S BOOK LIST
(IN CORRECT READING ORDER)

HOT DAMNED SERIES
Fashionably Dead
Fashionably Dead Down Under
Hell on Heels
Fashionably Dead in Diapers
A Fashionably Dead Christmas
Fashionably Hotter Than Hell
Fashionably Dead and Wed
Fashionably Fanged
Fashionably Flawed
A Fashionably Dead Diary
Fashionably Forever After
Fashionably Fabulous
A Fashionable Fiasco
Fashionably Fooled
Fashionably Dead and Loving It
Fashionably Dead and Demonic
The Oh My Gawd Couple

GOOD TO THE LAST DEATH SERIES
It's a Wonderful Midlife Crisis
Whose Midlife Crisis Is It Anyway?
A Most Excellent Midlife Crisis
My Midlife Crisis, My Rules
You Light Up My Midlife Crisis
It's A Matter of Midlife and Death
The Facts of Midlife

MY SO CALLED MYSTICAL MIDLIFE SERIES
The Write Hook
You May Be Write
All the Write Moves

SHIFT HAPPENS SERIES
Ready to Were
Some Were in Time
No Were To Run
Were Me Out
Were We Belong

MAGIC AND MAYHEM SERIES
Switching Hour
Witch Glitch
A Witch in Time
Magically Delicious
A Tale of Two Witches
Three's A Charm
Switching Witches
You're Broom or Mine?
The Bad Boys of Assjacket

The Newly Witch Game

SEA SHENANIGANS SERIES
Tallulah's Temptation
Ariel's Antics
Misty's Mayhem
Petunia's Pandemonium
Jingle Me Balls

A WYLDE PARANORMAL SERIES
Beauty Loves the Beast

HANDCUFFS AND HAPPILY EVER AFTERS SERIES
How Hard Can it Be?
Size Matters
Cop a Feel

If after reading all the above you are still wanting more
adventure and zany fun, read *Pirate Dave and His Randy
Adventures*, the romance novel budding novelist Rena helped
wicked Evangeline write in *How Hard Can It Be*?

Warning: Pirate Dave Contains Romance Satire, Spoofing,
and Pirates with Two Pork Swords.

NOTE FROM THE AUTHOR

If you enjoyed reading *Madison's Mess,* please consider leaving a positive review or rating on the site where you purchased it. Reader reviews help my books continue to be valued by resellers and help new readers make decisions about reading them.

You are the reason I write these stories and I sincerely appreciate each of you!

Many thanks for your support,
~ Robyn Peterman

Want to hear about my new releases?
Visit robynpeterman.com and join my newsletter!

ABOUT ROBYN PETERMAN

Robyn Peterman writes because the people inside her head won't leave her alone until she gives them life on paper. Her addictions include laughing really hard with friends, shoes (the expensive kind), Target, iced coffee with a squirt of chocolate syrup and extra ice in a Yeti cup, bejeweled reading glasses, her kids, her super-hot hubby and collecting stray animals.

A former professional actress with Broadway, film and T.V. credits, she now lives in the South with her family and too many animals to count.

Writing gives her peace and makes her whole, plus having a job where she can work in her sweatpants works really well for her.